Aquarian Amazon

Cate Cummings
Publicity & Promotion Group
7601 East 93rd Street
Kansas City, MO 64138-4206
(816) 767-0396 • Fax (816) 767-0289
Email: Cor@BookPublicity.com
Website: www.BookPublicity.com

Also by Anneliese Widman, Ph.D.

MY FEMALE, MY MALE, MY SELF and GOD:
A Modern Woman in Search of Her Soul

RAGE AT GOD:
Ascending to Reunion

Aquarian Amazon

Anneliese Widman, Ph.D.

Pentland Press, Inc.
www.pentlandpressusa.com

PUBLISHED BY PENTLAND PRESS, INC.
5122 Bur Oak Circle, Raleigh, North Carolina 27612
United States of America
919-782-0281

Library of Congress Control Number: 00-133642

Printed in the United States of America

Dedicated to . . .

. . . those readers of *Aquarian Amazon* who believe as I do, that the female/male selves are in each one of us, influenced by our parents and our environment.

When we dispense with the parental influences and dig underneath the surface for our true identity, we will find our amazing Godself. When we have cleared away the debris of unwanted masks and unnecessary outer apparel and stand naked before our Maker, we will realize that Divinity, too, is female/male. Were we not made in that Image?

Even Jesus gave credence to such a fact when, in the Gospel of Thomas (*The Secret Teachings of Jesus*; Marvin W. Meyer, trans.), He said:

> *When you make the two into one,*
> *when you make the inner like the outer*
> *   and the outer like the inner,*
> *   and the upper like the lower,*
> *when you make male and female*
> *   into a single one,*
> *so that the male will not be male*
> *and the female will not be female,*
> *. . . . .*
> *then you will enter the kingdom.*

Contents

Part Three

Preface

Aquarian Amazon is a tale from many sources. Kendra's and Ronald's numerous adventures combine my own experiences with those of clients in my professional psychotherapeutic practice, who also are on a quest for wholeness. The heroine, Kendra, is a composite of other women and myself. Likewise, Ronald is a composite of several different men.

Aquarian Amazon is an outgrowth of my lifelong interest in the female/male relationship. As a child I stared at couples, desperately trying to intuit the mystery of their togetherness. I never aspired to become part of an ordinary couple—no, only of a couple where each partner was an entity unto herself or himself, creating a whole that, when balanced, would fuse with the Godself. When I became an accomplished dancer, I made my search for this relationship the subject of my dances, always wondering how two became one.

The process of clarifying the concepts for *Aquarian Amazon* was an exciting one. I used the idea of female/male energies in one's being, which I elucidated in my first book, *My Female, My Male, My Self, and God: A Modern Woman in Search of Her Soul*. From that same work, I also used the concept of *Reflectivism*, which I covered further in my second book, *Rage at God: Ascending to Reunion*. In *Aquarian Amazon* I expand the methodology of *Imaging*, which I also wrote about in my first book. All of my books incorporate past lives as powerful aspects of the growth process.

Through Kendra's and Ronald's search, *Aquarian Amazon* chronicles a journey toward balance of the female and male natures. Kendra personifies a soul that "goes for it" fully. She's driven to do it all in this lifetime. Ronald is an example of another soul, in this case a male, who is not that driven and is comfortable with his neuroses, more fearful of confrontation with himself than of stagnation. The neurotic aspects of each personality are emphasized because these aspects need rectification—that is, to be made conscious, cleared away, and balanced.

I have been inspired to work with the concept of female/male energies because the balancing of these energies will truly create wholeness. If these two energies in one's being are not addressed (and this is not done in the majority of psychological modalities), the person will continue to flounder, remain incomplete, and look to the other sex for wholeness. Such a state will perpetuate the war of the sexes.

In the introduction of my first book I express this urgent need when I say, "I have not left a stone unturned to find the balance that I seek." I have often wondered: Is this my mission in this life . . . to find that balance, to live from it, to impart this information to other women and men, so that when balanced, they—as well as I—can reach the Godself? Is this not the purpose for coming to this planet—to work our karma through so we can return to our essence and, if qualified, do more elevated work in the heavenly spheres than what is possible on the Earth?

I've asked myself another question: Why now? The answer: Now my soul is readier than in any previous incarnation. My soul has the strength, the wisdom, the perseverance to plow through many obstacles—all in the quest for wholeness. For what purpose? To join the Godself.

Kendra is such a soul. By story's end, she truly has become an Amazon for the new age—an Aquarian Amazon. I believe that many women today are joining her.

My fondest wish for this book is that it will give you, the reader, tools and inspiration you can use to begin or deepen your own journey toward balance, freedom, and wholeness.

Part One

Kendra's Prayer

Oh, Universe,
Thou art bountiful!

Send me a mate who
can love me,
and whom I can love.

Above everything,
let us be right for
one another.

You know what my past
has been.
You know better than I
whom to send.

Amen.

I ended my prayer—one I have been praying for the last two years. How will the universe—that all-wise and all-knowing universe—answer it?

1
God, Send Me a Mate

He cradled me in his arms and rocked me. My breasts were pressed against his chest, my face nuzzled into the opening of his shirt, against his skin. I felt the smoothness of his skin, smelled his smell. I breathed it in until I realized I had put my arms around him, pressing closer, ever closer to him. He gathered my legs to his body and enveloped me so completely that no space remained between us. His face rested against my head. I asked myself, Why does he feel so familiar, so comfortable to be with?

We were alone in a basement room of my home, in the midst of a bodywork session. As my body rocked to and fro, my thoughts turned to the path that had led me to this moment.

A few years ago, I had sat on the edge of my bed, pleading with God to send me a mate. In a short time, God did.

I met him in a professional seminar. We peered at each other through a tall window, I on the inside, he on the outside. As he looked at me looking at him, a sudden grin creased his face. That was the beginning.

We were both ecstatic. I thought to myself, He is God-sent. I've been heard!

He was younger than I. I was readier than he for a serious relationship and for a child. Even though we were synchronized in uncanny ways, he didn't want a child; he wasn't as emotionally developed as I had hoped.

We grew apart. I, bitter and exhausted from the ordeal of relating, became celibate, a workaholic. I learned a great deal during this period. I felt no sexual stirring for another man. I was not asexual, hardly that. I was still a handful, an energy that could engage a man completely. I concentrated on my work as a psychotherapist, helping others grow as I also grew.

For a number of years I intentionally abstained from having a love relationship, realizing I did not welcome any more mistakes—misjudgments that were painful for the man as well as for me. I sensed that further growth was necessary to connect to that other gender in a balanced way. But what kind of growth? What was missing? The matter remained a mystery. I knew that in my dealings with men, my nature had been either tyrannical or caretaking. Neither quality had any resemblance to love. I then prayed my prayer. Slowly, answers came—answers that were a revelation and provided clarity.

The first of these revelations occurred two years ago, when a sensuous, earthy man who worked on my property in the country brought me back to life. He instinctively felt my sensual nature and responded with his own. Suddenly, my dormant sexual self was smitten.

I woke with a start. When I did, he conveniently disappeared—said he had other things to do.

Did You send him, God, to waken me and pass on?

Did my sexuality go to sleep again? No, the yearning continued to spread like wildfire through my body. I began to long to be enfolded by the man and joined with him. Oh, God, You know how these feelings can consume a person. This sexual energy demonstrated again and again why it had been named "serpent energy" by the ancient ones. It did not stay dormant but remained coiled, wakeful, at the base of my spine. It stretched deliberately, lustfully, even though I attempted to keep it under control. And I managed to keep it under control—until last August.

I had taken a year-long sabbatical from my psychotherapeutic practice. The month was hot; I stayed inside my cool house writing, an activity that was taking up more and more of my new luxury of free time. I kept two computer files open simultaneously. In one, intensely personal, I played with the therapeutic aspects of laying straight a welter of past feelings and experiences that I felt a strong need to deal with more completely and finally resolve. The second file, a fictionalized account of those experiences, offered me a creative release and helped me discover, by looking through the characters' eyes, choices I might have made in my own life if I had been aware of them at the time. It was fascinating to make these discoveries.

I took a leap of faith and mailed a book proposal to a literary agent, along with a couple of those chapters. To my great surprise I received a request to submit as much writing as I had already done on the story. She liked what I sent her enough to phone me with a deadline to draw the story to a close, explaining that she wanted to submit the work to publishers as soon as possible. I was deeply excited as well as agitated. This state and my need to have a mate must have intensified the uncoiling serpent, which continued to travel up my spine. As it did so, my vertebrae went out of alignment. In pain, I sought a chiropractor. He made the proper adjustment, but this persistent energy, not to be denied, disrupted my spine again and again. To cope with the pain, various muscle groups throughout my body took on the stress.

Someone referred me to a healer. He came to my house. Ronald was about fifty, five years older than I, a practitioner whose work was similar to Bioenergetics, the therapeutic modality I had used in my own practice. His massage techniques were familiar, but he used them in ways I had never before encountered. I was both excited and connected to what he was doing.

Ronald had brown hair and was of medium height, with a lean figure and a striking face. I noticed nothing more about him; I was focused on my pain and lowered myself willingly onto the carpeted floor for the treatment.

As he worked on my body, I was surprised at how much my energy had diminished, allowing so much stress to accumulate, and how much I had neglected my body and its needs. His hands felt good as he touched the areas that needed to be manipulated. Session after session, the pain lessened as he massaged muscle, bone, tissue. Then something more happened.

His blue eyes twinkled mischievously as my body became more alive. The serpent continued to uncoil steadily, and soon my pelvis felt on fire. I told myself this was due to the summer heat. But was it? I ignored the answer. In the meantime his hands continued to move skillfully over my hurting muscles; the tension left and with it, my pain.

Over the weeks my body grew to ache for his touch. Sometimes his fingers slipped when manipulating the muscles on the inside of my thighs, an area that so often holds suppressed tension. I would become alert, hold my breath, and wait for what he would do next. He would linger on one spot. I thought he was lingering a bit too long, but I convinced myself that there must be a muscular knot in that area, and that by persistently massaging the knot, he would soon dissolve it.

"Hmm," he said, as he took away his hands. "Hmm."

I asked, "Why 'hmm'?"

"Just hmm," he repeated, as he pulled up my sweat pants, which I had lowered earlier to expose the hurting area.

We rose from the floor. He knelt before me as he manipulated the muscles between my thighs. I began shaking involuntarily. He said the shaking was an energy release. My mind silently called it by its technical name: *clonism*. I said nothing, intent on enjoying the disappearance of my tension.

"This is good," he muttered, massaging my inner thighs, groin, and buttocks, as the shaking continued. I wallowed in his approach, never having experienced so much release of tension with so much intensity throughout my entire body so quickly. Slightly apprehensive, however, I asked him between involuntary jerks, "Are you sure this is good?"

"I'm sure," he smiled.

As he spoke I felt a warmth enter my solar plexus like a bolt of lightning. I gasped.

"Will it ever stop?" I wondered aloud as I bobbed up and down, up and down in one spot. He assured me that it would, as he anchored my feet with his hands.

Before long, it did stop. And I felt the hot fire of serpent energy surge through my body as I had never felt it before.

He rose and stood before me. I looked into his blue eyes; he met my gaze. Was it an hour or a second? I don't know.

He broke the silence. "I feel so connected to you."

I stood there and smiled, inwardly ecstatic. He looked away, then whispered, "I'll come back tomorrow."

Several hours after his departure I took my newly alive, yearning body and psyche to bed, where I dreamed a lovely dream. I don't remember more than that—only that it felt lovely.

2
The Healer

The next day, a rainy one, was dominated by memories of the energy between us. My pelvis smoldered steadily from the fire that had been ignited. "Oh, God!" I sighed, "this feeling is so delicious . . . so sweet. Can there be anything sweeter in Your creation, Lord? What else do You have in store for me?"

Ronald had wanted me to keep the entry door unlocked at the anticipated time of his visit. He said he didn't want to stand in the rain waiting for me to answer the doorbell. When he first made this request, I balked before agreeing. I was afraid that if he suddenly appeared in the house I wouldn't be prepared.

"Prepared?" I asked myself. Prepared for what? Prepared to hide the feelings that seeing him brought to my heart and body? But why should these feelings be hidden?

He might not feel the same as I do . . . he might be married, were my responses. All right, I told myself, be controlled. Why be vulnerable needlessly?

I heard the wheels of his car crunch on the pebbled driveway. Soon I heard his footsteps in the basement, the room in which we had worked. He called, "Kendra." My name never sounded so melodious. I took three deep breaths and answered, "Hi. I'll be right down." As I descended the staircase, Ronald was at the bottom of it, waiting.

His blue eyes scanned my eyes, then my body, while he took my hand.

Once again he knelt before me, putting one hand between my thighs, the other on my feet to ground my energy and connect me to my body so I could take in the treatment more effectively. I felt his body breathing heavily, like mine. He rose to his feet. We looked into one another's eyes.

"You look so tired and pale," I said. "What's happened since yesterday?"

His eyes became misty; I realized they were tearing. He mastered his feelings, and his tears vanished. With a heart-tugging little chuckle he explained, "I get like this when I feel connected to someone."

I thought, He feels as I do! So, then, why doesn't he let his feelings show?

He's a professional! my mind retorted. He's here to give me a session, not to make a personal confession.

I coolly told him that I was experiencing a great deal of tension in my chest, back, and shoulder girdle. He instructed me to remove my shirt.

"What?"

"I have to see your structure and flesh in order to work adequately."

Remembrance of some of the Bioenergetic techniques, in which an unclothed body was essential, flooded back. "Oh. Yes, of course."

He gently but firmly began to remove my sweatshirt. He had trouble getting my arms out of the sleeves and asked for my assistance. I struggled with the tight wrist bands. In a short time I found myself half naked.

I lay on my back, pleading to God to turn me into a Venus, to instantly waft away the effects of too many ice cream treats I'd consumed during the recent weeks.

He palpated my chest and instructed me to breathe deeply so the structure of my chest would move visibly. I did what he asked but when my chest moved only slightly, I looked at him helplessly, feeling like a complete failure.

He looked into my eyes and with great earnestness told me, "Breathing will create feelings and movement. If you drop your jaw while you're breathing, the air will fill your chest and lungs, and you'll soon experience another reality."

It all sounded familiar, but I felt inhibited. I was so vulnerable in my half-naked state. Finally, I breathed hard with my jaw loose and open. I hyperventilated, thus succeeding too well. I lost awareness. I went elsewhere—to a place of no particular dimension, just elsewhere.

The next thing I was aware of was my head being moved from side to side. My eyes met Ronald's as I struggled back to reality.

"What happened?" he asked.

"I don't know," I answered blankly.

He urged me to remember. I puckered up my face, put my arms over my eyes, and said in a childish voice, "No, I don't want to. It's too painful."

"Ah," he said alertly. "So you *did* go somewhere. You've lived through some feelings. What were they?"

"I don't know. And I don't want to know," I answered petulantly.

With a slight grin he finished my thought, "So there!"

Even in my half-present condition, I had to laugh at his response. He waited for my laughter to subside, then asked softly, "How old are you?"

I no longer felt like a failure but like a detective in search of a vital clue. I breathed hard again, mouth ajar. "Seventeen," I said fretfully, as memories—vague, dark memories—rose before me. Sobs broke forth from my body, sobs I had never anticipated, tucked away in what seemed to be the most hidden place in the core of my being.

He gathered my body into his arms, my face nuzzled into the opening of his shirt. I smelled his smell. I breathed it in until my brain let go of my surroundings, my body following, floating in space. We clung together, propelled by God's energy to a destination that would give us learning and wisdom about ourselves. This was a holy gift for Ronald's consciousness and mine, to bring us ever closer to our souls.

We breathed deeply and slowly together. Our breathing began to synchronize. Our highest energy centers opened as we fused into one being. A sound like a waterfall . . . then a rainbow of liquid colors resolved into a scene that was new yet very familiar. Reality was transformed as we entered another world. A very real, very living world.

The way I sense my body has become different. I realize that I do not look the same. I am younger and so graceful and beautiful. My skin is dark, like my black, wavy hair, which falls far down my back. The man by my side is handsome, his hair blond, his skin smooth, his muscles long and firm. He has blue eyes. The same blue eyes.

We are both naked. We have just loved one another passionately. He's cradling and rocking my body, which we know holds our child.

He alternately touches my round abdomen and kisses my full breasts. I release myself gently from his embrace to look at his face, but he quickly pulls me to his chest, taking time to gain control of his feelings. I'm delighted he is so happy.

Soon I insist on looking into his eyes. As his gaze meets mine, we melt into one another, overtaken by an ecstasy that drives us to quench our thirst for one another again, uniting again and again in love. Our passion is boundless.

We are finally quiet, drenched in perspiration from our love-making. I sit up beside him in the dark hut. "I'll go to the queen and explain our situation."

He places his fingers on my lips, wanting nothing to interrupt the bliss between us. Aware of every nuance of his moods, I want only to ease whatever worries fill his mind. Gently I seek to reassure him. I whisper softly, kissing his neck, "Don't despair, Sedeth. The queen will give us permission to keep the child." *Then, almost as a forbidden afterthought,* "As well as permission to wed."

He looks at me tenderly, then shakes his head. "I don't trust her as you do," *he finally mutters.* "I'm a slave. Consent for you and me to marry would anger all the Amazon women. The queen wants the community to remain as it is—strictly matriarchal. If she made this concession for you, the other women, too, would demand their own mates. Inevitably that would enhance the status of all men, even if only slightly. You know the queen is too selfish to relinquish that much of her power."

His matter-of-fact presentation of the reality of our situation makes me feel frantic. "But she's always cared for me personally," *I argue.* "Maybe she'll make an exception. After all, she helped raise me. She came to love and admire my mother and even became my guardian after my mother died."

"I'm not convinced that your queen is capable of that much sentiment. You would have to be very, very special to her for that to make a difference. How did she come to raise you?"

I am surprised that Sedeth and I had never discussed my beginnings in the matriarchy. "I've never told you how my mother came to be here?"

"No," *replies Sedeth.* "Somehow it never seemed important before. Now it seems of great importance to me. How did she get here?"

"This is the story the queen told me over and over again when I was a child. My mother was a noblewoman, married to a tyrant of a man who kept her locked in her room because she was pregnant. He wouldn't look upon what he considered her disfigurement. He wanted a child but was interested only in the final product, the child itself. The birth travail would be endured by her with the help of the servants, while he waited outside the birthing room for a male child. She was expected to reappear shortly after the birth, slim and attractive as before, ready to indulge his whims.

"When she was four months pregnant with me, the Amazons pillaged her town and found her locked in her room. When she saw the queen, she held her arms out to her and begged to join the matriarchy. 'Please take me with you. I'm tired of living in a world where men can be so cruel to women.'

"You can imagine, Sedeth, how the queen relished telling me this story. She tells it with pride that her warrior women raided our village successfully and that a noblewoman like my mother felt the same way about men as she does."

"You mean how insanely hateful she feels toward them?" is Sedeth's disgusted response.

"Yes," I agree, "but I know that my mother was capable of much more compassion and made many subtle efforts to influence the queen's attitudes."

Sedeth simply grunts. I laugh and continue with my story.

"The queen welcomed her and brought her to this community, where she gave birth to me five months later. My mother was forever grateful to the queen, whose friend and companion she became. When I was ten years old, my mother knew her death was near and made the queen my guardian. From the day she died, the queen raised me as her own.

"So you see, Sedeth," I conclude, "I'm the closest thing to a child the queen will ever have. She has to listen to me differently than she would listen to another woman. I can go to her and plead with her to let us remain together. I can tell her we'll live outside of the community, so no one will know."

He listens attentively, but his blue eyes darken.

"Nur, you know the facts as well as I do. We've been together as lovers for three years, the maximum allowed time for the women of your tribe. At the full moon you'll be assigned another slave-lover. I'll be assigned to another woman. We'll be parted forever. Perhaps out of love for your mother, the queen will let you keep our child. Perhaps not. She's a woman of strong, unpredictable impulses."

I feel the coldness creep into his heart as he reminds me of the circumstances of our lives. I press my body so close to his, we become as one breath, and he feels my terror and pain.

I cry and cry. "You are my true beloved, Sedeth. No one can part us! It would be a violation of Nature. The queen will understand that we're made of one cloth, that it was ordained by the Mother Goddess for us to be together. I'll go to her, tell her how we feel, ask her for permission to remain together." *In desperation I fling out one arm, gesturing with it as though to strengthen my resolve.*

"No, I must beg her, even to the point of humiliation. I don't wish to live without you and our child!"

Deeply affected by my love for him, he smiles and pushes me away from him to see me more clearly. He wipes away my tears and plants sweet kisses over my eyes and nose and lips. "You are so beautiful, Nur."

His face brightens suddenly as he reminds me of our first meeting. "Three years ago, when I first saw you, my rage at my powerless state began to melt. As the queen's attendants assigned us to one another, my eyes feasted secretly on you. I knew then that you were my beloved. I knew that if I weren't a slave and we were able to live as free people, I still would instantly have known you from among all women as the one who is the other half of me."

I listen, eagerly soaking in his words, wanting the moments together to be everlasting.

He pauses, recalling that time, then murmurs, "Do you remember our first night together? Do you remember how frightened you were? How you tried to be cold, aloof, and commanding? You tried to apply the sexual rules you had been taught since you were a young girl to your newly assigned slave."

I am so embarrassed that I hide my face on his chest.

Sedeth strokes my hair. "I saw what you were doing and smiled inside. When I approached you, do you recall how you blushed scarlet through your dark skin?"

I nod my head, remembering. "I was so innocent," *I think. I am glad that Sedeth is stroking my hair. It takes the attention away from the embarrassment I feel, even at this moment.*

"I'll confess to you now that my heart throbbed at your beauty and innocence. I also tried to appear cold and aloof. My duty as a slave was to perform the sexual act well and to win your favor; otherwise I might be killed, or delegated to do the most menial tasks.

"But much as I tried to remain a distant sexual object," he continues, "I wanted to fulfill whatever desires you had. I couldn't be other than gentle and loving. My body felt complete when I touched you, when I was inside you; complete, when I was near your energy.

"Oh, Nur!" Sedeth says fervently. "I couldn't get enough of you from the very beginning. I was your first sexual experience; all my sensibilities screamed out to me to cherish this beautiful, young maiden. My soul was speaking to me." He looks at me and shakes his head in wonder. "You are today as you were then: yearning, loving, trusting. I could never have hurt you; I could never have plundered your virginal state vengefully, as I know other captives do with their assigned women. As a result, you grew to love me."

I listen intently. Oh, Mother Goddess, I plead silently, let nothing come between us.

"Surely you must know that as slaves, all the men are filled with rage at our captivity and at the women we must serve. Even though we scheme and plot among ourselves how to become free, none of us has managed to escape. I often wonder if the opportunity to escape presented itself now whether I would take it."

Sedeth lifts my face with his hands and looks into my eyes. "I know I wouldn't. Because I love you, Nur. At first in spite of myself, but now with my whole heart."

Oh, God—I, Kendra, thought with the tiny part of my consciousness that was not immersed in my life as Nur in the Amazon period. I was beautiful, charming, inviting, not the ugly person my mother has told me I am ever since my birth into this life. Catch up, Kendra, catch up.

I, Nur, also remember the time three years ago when Sedeth, my love, had first been captured. I was seventeen. I had been in my hut when the queen's attendants came to tell me I was to be mated with my first slave.

I was bewildered at first, because under the protection of the queen, my life had been sheltered. She had looked on me favorably, and I was well taken care of by her servants and taught the important skills: hunting, self-defense, and midwifery.

One day the queen discovered me singing while doing my chores. At her command I was taught the proper use of my voice. Thereafter I sang at special events, such as the birth of a female child, the capture of a wild animal, and the celebration of the strength of women. My voice grew sweeter and sweeter as my body developed, and my yearning for fulfillment became deeper and more intense.

"Do you remember, Sedeth? You heard my voice when you approached my hut. I was brushing my hair and singing to the spirits to bring me a pleasing mate. When I looked up and beheld you standing before me, I thought I saw a god.

"I knelt before you as you entered the hut. Wisely you pulled me to my feet. It was then I regained my composure and attempted to apply the rules of the tribe. How awkward I was in your presence, and how the corners of your mouth twitched with laughter.

"You asked me to continue singing. I shook my bowed head from side to side like a child. I placed my right foot on top of the left, then reversed my feet as I became more embarrassed. Oh, my love, how ill at ease I was in the presence of a handsome man; how nervous to be before a man at all!

"To put me at ease, you sat before me on the mat, looked into my face, and kindly and gently urged me to sing again. Even in my awkward state, I felt that you were like a king upon whom I would bestow the most beautiful gift, if only I could muster the courage to sing.

"Finally, the courage came. As you gazed upon me, I breathed fully into my body. My heart expanded and my throat responded like a nightingale's. I sang with all my heart. I've sung this song to you repeatedly since then. I've whispered it into your ears or hummed it quietly while we worked in the fields.

> My desire for a true,
> true mate
> brings tears to my eyes.
> My soul urges me forward.
>
> I yearn for him
> with an unceasing
> love
> that needs
> to be satisfied.

My heart then
becomes quiet.

Ecstasy is ours.
Two become one.
One never again two.
Living—
is
complete.

"I remember it all, my lovely Nur," Sedeth answers softly. "But we must face the other events that are not so pleasant."

I must admit, God, that I resist being reminded of our terrible dilemma. I would rather reminisce forever, cradled in Sedeth's arms, feeling only the joy and love between us.

A man loved me deeply and I loved him. The possibility to love that way is within me. What happened to that capacity?

Sedeth pulls away from me, then takes my hands in a strong grip; his eyes have a storm in them. His grasp becomes fierce. Tears well up in my eyes.

"Remember! Remember!" he rages. "Remember Ariane and Preder!"

I remember: Ariane was nineteen when Preder, her lover of three years, was assigned to a new woman. They went to the queen with their plea to remain together. She listened to them both.

"How could a woman of our community become so helplessly involved with a mere man?" she shouted as she spat on them both, then dismissed them. In their hut they waited for the queen's verdict.

"Remember!" is Sedeth's overpowering command as he grips my hand forcefully.

"Have you forgotten how Ariane's body was pulled out of her hut by the warrior women—immobilized by terror, her eyes bulging, her mouth open? Have you forgotten Ariane and Preder lying side by side on their bellies, their hands and legs tied behind them as is done with animals about to be slaughtered? Have you forgotten your queen, attired as though for entry into battle, standing before them, giving the command to her warrior women to tear them limb from limb? Have you forgotten that the entire community let out a howl of horror?

"Your own knees buckled and you fainted in the dirt."

3
We Go Somewhere

The grandfather clock in the basement room struck six. The chimes, melodious and insistent, had played a long prelude before the emphatic, hammerlike announcement. Ronald and I were entwined in each other's arms. I awakened slowly from the trancelike state, weeping. He gestured hazily, trying to raise me from the floor.

Ronald separated himself from me abruptly and looked at his watch. Softly he told me he had to leave. "What?" I asked, still in a daze.

"I have to leave. I'm expected to make supper tonight for my wife and a few friends," he explained, all the while eyeing me carefully.

"Oh," I said, shocked, but covering my reaction. "Well, hand me my sweatshirt."

He gently pulled the shirt over my head. Our eyes met. He placed two sweet, delicate kisses on both sides of my mouth.

I wanted more. I wanted the fullness of his lips. Still resonating from Sedeth's and Nur's love for one another, I lifted my face with an expectation of greater passion. He rose swiftly to his feet, helped me to mine. Before I could say a word, he was gone.

I stood alone in the doorway, looking out into the garden. Absently I watched the activity at two bird feeders in the distance. The birds were busily flying from one feeder to the other, their bills filled with the luscious seeds. After a tasty meal, they groomed themselves attentively before embarking on a flight for another beakful of elixir.

"You know what satisfaction is, don't you, little feathery creatures."

I went to the door to lock it, arguing mentally with the absent Ronald. I'm here. But where are you? I've had an amazing experience. What about you? You bolted out of here as though you'd been summoned by a queen. This thought stopped me dead. I asked myself, A queen from this life—or the ancient one?

I'm going crazy, I thought. I'm beginning to waver between what's real and what's from the "past." There was no doubt in my mind that the scenes now etched with such clarity in my conscious memory were indeed myself and Ronald many ages ago. Ronald, how could you just disappear like that, leaving me so unsettled?

I watched the birds a while longer, envious of their simple existence, baffled by my profound, disturbing experience. My body was in a state of disorder and yearning. God! What was happening to me? Is this Your answer to my prayer? A married man? One with a six o'clock curfew? I couldn't help but laugh at myself at this remark.

The phone rang. It was Ronald. He apologized for leaving so abruptly. He wondered if we could extend our next session, scheduled for the following day, to give us enough time to talk.

"Of course," I mumbled.

The phone was on fire at both ends. I felt the electric current from him come through me. My heart pounded. I wanted to scream, to cry, to plead with him to chuck his appointment with his wife and friends then return to be with me so I could hold him and be held, to say nothing, to say everything. Most important, simply to be held and to breathe with him.

Despite the electricity between us, he remained masterfully in control, almost detached. Buddhist training? I wondered. He had mentioned that he was a devotee of that discipline.

"You're so detached," I managed to gasp between the shivers that raced through my body.

"Do you want me to be attached?" he asked skillfully.

"No," I said quickly. "Just be yourself."

I chuckled, feeling I had the upper hand. While I had it, I ended our conversation, "I'll see you tomorrow. Good night."

"Good night," he said hesitantly, then hung up.

I stood before the phone as though I had been embraced. "What is happening?" I shouted to the heavens. "Where is this going?" I thought: it can't go anywhere. He's married! But the feelings when we're together are so sweet! I can't give them up now, not yet. Let me go to sleep and dream and wait for tomorrow.

I slept that night. There must have been a smile on my face for the next blissful, dreamy eight hours. But an underlying turbulence lay at the base of my unconscious. I awakened the next day feeling sweet and sour, bright and dark. I felt torn asunder from the previous day's experiences, both with Ronald and with Sedeth. I forced myself to sit at my computer and put my attention on the writing that had to be done.

I knew we needed to talk. Today!

4
We Need to Talk

I resolved that the basement door would remain locked.

Ronald hadn't warned me yesterday about having to leave at a specific time. So why should I accommodate him so easily? Let him knock and wait. Let him stand in the rain, the snow, in the blasting heat. Let his masculine ego tarnish a bit as he waits. Let him stand helplessly in the elements until the woman is ready to open the door.

I thought, Let you in? I've let you in too much. I don't have the detached defensiveness that keeps you cool and casual. You'll not get in again, not so easily.

I had seven hours ahead of me to do the work I had planned. The sun rose to its height and slowly slipped beyond the zenith. I was immersed in my assignment, proud that I was not ruminating about him, that I was in control of my emotions.

As the time of our meeting approached, I discovered that my feelings and my body had a life of their own. My determined ego-resolve evaporated as strong cramps developed in my abdomen. I sat in agony for a while, until it occurred to me to investigate this unexpected onslaught of pain. I realized that I felt anxious about keeping the door locked. I felt anxious that Ronald might leave and I would never see him again. I was anxious that I might be pushing men away, acting from an unconscious, unbridled rage toward them. I did understand, however, that this behavior was a residue of very early experiences with my father, who also had not been available to me.

Whatever the outcome of this relationship would be, I thought, I didn't want to subject a man to my usual tyrannical behavior; yet I didn't want to put myself into a victimized position, either, one that camouflaged my punitive tendencies. I felt determined to change old patterns, striving for a balance between the two extremes.

I made a decision. A few minutes before Ronald's scheduled arrival, I went to the basement door to unlock it. I smiled as I saw the busy activity of the birds. I was again envious of the simplicity of their existence, particularly since I had to face this difficult meeting.

As I opened the latch of the door, I received comfort from the thought that, in time, I would know if unlocking the door, a gesture not only real but symbolic, was the right action for me to have taken. I had no deeper grasp of the matter than this. I was convinced, however, that by leaving the door open, my psyche was neither vindictive nor victimized. If being open led to pain, I knew that this time I would not be prostrated by it.

I returned to my computer. My heart beat rapidly. I sensed his approach. I restrained my excitement, determined to stay in control. I busied myself with printing what I had written that day.

I was editing the pages when I felt the energy in the room change. A glow, a hot, effervescent radiance invaded my energy field. Without looking up, I felt Ronald standing by my side, watching me shut down the computer.

We smiled enigmatically. He leaned over and kissed both sides of my mouth. In an instant, my earlier ruminating became meaningless, along with my earlier resolves. I entered the flow between us willingly.

We stayed in the computer room. He brought me into the center of the floor, where he began to work with my body. Kneeling with his hands between my thighs, opening the energy flow to my legs and feet, he gazed at me with his blue eyes. I felt his longing to hold me and touch me in a way that was beyond the requirements of his professional healing techniques. He restrained his impulses, however.

I was aglow. We were two sparks of energy ignited, and there was nothing we could do about it. My mind did not obey me; his mind did not obey him.

He instructed me to lie on my back. Before I sank to the floor, I voluntarily took off my shirt. At first he kneaded my shoulders and upper back gently, then more insistently, until I cried out from the unbearable muscular pain. I thrashed about, trying to avoid his pressure against my supertight musculature.

He stopped working, wondering out loud if I wanted him to continue or did I want to rest. I lay down and asked him to lie on top of my body, his chest on mine, his hands cupping the back of my head. When he complied, I sighed like an infant, finally getting warmth and comforting.

I looked into his blue eyes. He avoided my gaze, putting his cheek next to mine. We breathed together. I felt us meld into one another.

He began to breathe heavily. I suggested he resume working. He smiled knowingly at me and lifted himself off my body. Before he rose, however, he placed his two hands over my breasts as though sculpting them.

I looked at him quizzically, questioning his motivation.

"It's part of the massage," he said. He then pulled them together and kissed them lightly before he resumed his position above my head that gave him access to my shoulders and back.

So, I thought to myself. He's in a playful mood. You scoundrel, you know so well how to play with me. But your touch on my breasts is so delicious, so subtly teasing. I wonder if this is what it would be like to consummate our passion. But not with a married man!

"Ouch!" I hollered as the pain of the manipulation brought me back to the moment. He dug into the tight muscles with added zeal, until I pleaded, "Enough! Give me a rest!"

Ronald stopped. Again he climbed on top of my body, holding my head as before, his cheek against my cheek.

"Who gave you permission to climb on top of me again?" I asked, feigning innocence.

"You did, didn't you?" he answered playfully. "I'll get off if it makes you uncomfortable."

"Stay," I said. "I never realized how much I need to be held. You're playing with me, but I like it. Keep holding me."

"Yes, madam."

He brushed his lips lightly across mine.

I was suddenly a lusting animal, pulling his lips toward mine. We opened our mouths to one another, our tongues seeking, until the embrace felt complete, united. We rolled on our sides, entwined in each other's arms, each of us desiring to find entry into the other's soul.

I gave a lustful sob, as did he! He quieted me by telling me to breathe with him. I did. We did.

5

That Kind of Mystery

I went back to my happy memories. Now, safe in the comfort of our embrace, I surrendered to the lucent waterfall and went back where I wanted to be—to before our terrible fear, our dilemma. Sedeth's and Nur's.

A little more than two years after being mated with Sedeth, I was sent for by the queen to render my midwifery services. Lela, the pregnant woman, had been assigned to a slave at the same time Sedeth had come into my life.

I was aware that, unlike the union between Sedeth and me, Lela's relationship with her slave was one that followed the rules of the tribe perfectly. She controlled her lover, keeping him at a distance throughout their time together; he slept like a trained dog outside her hut, waiting for her next command. She was determined to procreate for the sake of increasing the population of the matriarchy and would call on his sexual services erratically, lapsing into moods of depression and fury when she discovered she was not pregnant. Her determination to bear a child made her lure him into her hut at odd times and frequently. Should he displease her or should his body be unresponsive to her needs, he would be beaten. He became an agitated, high-strung man, praying to the gods to make him fertile so he could serve his mistress and have some peace.

Lela's body finally showed the signs of a full womb. At first she was ecstatic. She knew that giving birth for the community would bring her the status of a valued member, but only if she bore a female child. She became obsessed about the gender of her offspring. She wrangled with her slave for hours, trying to extract from him information as to his genetic constitution. Did he have many sisters? Had he ever impregnated another woman? If so, what gender was the child?

Lela became a shrew. Her slave expressed to Sedeth and me his desire to run away, even at the cost of death. We restrained his impulse by reasoning with him. After the birth, we reminded him that he would have less than a year before being assigned to another mate. In the meantime, Lela would be occupied with the child and leave him alone.

I was rushed to the birthing hut at dawn. Lela writhed in agony on a mat on the ground. She cursed her slave. She cursed all men. They were the cause of her pains. She yelled at me to get "this thing" out of her. I urged her to push with each breath, but because she was a mixture of rage, terror, resentment, and confusion, her body fought against the natural progression of the contractions.

I finally saw the infant's head. With as much skill as I could muster, I pulled it out of her vagina. Her screams and failure to breathe hindered the process, but miraculously the infant came out of her body. It yelled loudly as it took its first breath.

Lela, exhausted, terrified, and bewildered, looked at the body that had just been expelled from hers. It was a boy! She turned her head away in disgust as I showed him to her, indicating that he should be placed on her breast to nurse.

She was resistant, unwelcoming to her newborn, wanting only to sleep. She was exhausted and disappointed. She was unhappy that the Mother Goddess had bestowed a male child on her and feared that now she would remain a nonentity in the community.

In the meantime, I placed the infant on his mother's breasts so he could get his nourishment. As he drank with gusto, Lela looked at this miracle with some interest. I thought I saw tenderness come into her eyes as she observed the features of the infant, the product of her crazed lovemaking.

I stayed with them throughout the day and night, making certain his nurturance was attended to. I felt that Lela was capable of a certain amount of bonding, but I also noticed that when she became aware of her openness to him, she quickly pushed him toward me. Then I would take him into my arms and sing to him, rocking him while I walked around the interior of the hut.

Lela watched me with wonder. She asked, "How do you know what to do? I don't know what to do next."

"Love tells you what to do next," I responded.

"What will happen to it when the queen discovers it's a boy?" she asked in a low voice. She knew as well as I did.

"I don't know," I answered, hoping against hope. "She may be more merciful than she has been at other times. Perhaps she will be more merciful."

I gave him back to Lela, who this time reached her arms out to receive him. I watched her bring him to her breasts as she welcomed his sucking.

Mother Goddess, I prayed silently, let no harm come to this little miracle. Put mercy into the queen's heart. At the very least, let her come to a decision before Lela loses herself in him.

Sedeth was waiting for me. He had cooked a meal, which I ate ravenously. I told him in detail of the experience. He stroked my hair and touched my body with his large warm hands. I stopped eating and fell into his arms, crying and pleading softly to him. "I want your child. I want your child. I want to see our love fulfilled in that kind of mystery. Love me now, this moment. Bring this joy into my womb."

"But what if it is a—" he questioned delicately, not finishing his sentence, overtaken by my passion.

"It doesn't matter. It doesn't matter," I said, pushing reality as far away as I could. "Nothing matters but that you enter me and love me."

He did. We were joined. This time I knew intuitively that his seed had taken hold and would grow inside me.

A love child: to be fused magically in love with the man. I've always wanted that. Why has it never happened?

"You're pregnant?" asked Ronald.

"Yes," I said, touching my abdomen. "You're finally inside me."

Ronald kissed my abdomen. He was gentle, loving, enthralled with the miracle of his sperm inside my womb, even though in truth it was Sedeth's sperm in Nur's womb. We were that involved with their story.

"You loved me so much," he said. "You loved me, knowing it might spell disaster. I loved you, too. It's a feeling I recognize now. It makes me melt. All I know is that I want to be entwined with you."

My belly has grown. I am more than halfway to my child's time of birth. We are in our hut. Sedeth dotes on me like a clucking hen. "Don't do that. Let me help you lift the water pails. Lie down, my beloved Nur, and rest." He sits beside me, stroking my abdomen, singing to the sleeping prince or princess inside my womb:

> *Cherished soul,*
> *conceived from love,*
> *grow in her welcoming womb.*
> *There has never been*
> *a moment of doubt*
> *that you are wanted by us.*

"That you are wanted by us," I chime in, laughing, delighting in his effort to create a song. He is slightly embarrassed, believing he could never match my vocal or creative abilities. I touch his cheek and tell him it is the most beautiful song I have ever heard.

6

The Crime:
A Male Child

The morning after Sedeth had composed his beautiful song, Lela appeared in the doorway of our hut, carrying her five-month-old son. She had bonded with him as intensely as she had wished to become pregnant and have a female child. Sedeth and I watched Lela nurse the infant, smothering him with her love.

We were taking turns holding him and doing all the things people do in admiration of a divine gift from the Mother Goddess, when Sedeth, with no forewarning, ran out of the hut and disappeared. I realized that holding the infant had brought forth terrible fears in him, not only for that child's future but also for our child's future.

Since the birth of her son, Lela had taken me into her confidence. With an urgency I knew had relevance to my own situation, I asked her if she had news about the queen's decision.

All three of us were aware that among the Amazons, male children were either killed or maimed. A crippled male growing up in a community of women would have little appeal for them, creating less risk of their forming a serious bond. Lela told me there was a rumor that the queen intended to call a meeting of all the non-warrior women, to have them make a collective decision about the fate of her son.

"What?" I asked, incredulous.

Lela repeated the rumor, hoping with all her heart that it would indeed be a reality. This way her son would have a chance to stay alive.

Upset and untrusting of the queen's motives, I quickly and secretly probed my memory. I recalled my last meeting with the monarch.

I had stood before her, well-balanced. I was a beautiful female. I carried Sedeth's child, giving me the aura of a full woman. As she scanned my body and looked into my eyes, I did not flinch. My eyes showed compassion for her lonely position in life, and I knew she *envied me. She envied the love of my man, who, in the eyes of the community, looked like a god. I reflected that she, too, could have the kind of joy I had, if only she would let her feminine nature shine forth from a beautiful, though neglected, body and soul.*

Her face beamed when she beheld me. "Sing to me, Nur," she entreated. "I've missed your voice and your healing hands." She paused for a moment. Her eyes narrowed. Uncharacteristically she confided, "I know you're angry at me for the deaths of Ariane and Preder. But I grow so strained. I must maintain order. I must hold to the principles of our community. Understand . . . do understand."

I was greatly surprised that she had spoken with such candor, and even though I wished to extend compassion to her, I was filled with sadness and revulsion at the determination she had made about the fate of my friends. I also knew too well that my own fate, and that of Sedeth, would rest on her decision now.

I sang as I massaged her arms and her back, but I sounded hoarse and raspy. Though I tried to sing the songs I had sung for many years, my voice—or rather my soul within my voice—had a life of its own and refused to repeat them. I was silent for a long time, until from deep within me my nightingale voice finally emerged. It emerged when I harnessed my courage and sang from the feelings inside my heart.

I sang about a leader who was not fanatical in her beliefs, who believed in her cause yet allowed her subjects to participate in decisions. I sang of justice, mercy, and love. I sang of the wisdom inside every being. I sang about her beauty and strength and her need to be loved, to submit to a man's love so she could achieve a divine balance. I sang of her warmth and generosity. I sang to the imprisoned woman inside her, whom she punished daily. I sang of my love for her. I sang of my disappointment and hurt when she acted without mercy.

I finally stopped. I had said it all. My heart and my conscience were purged. Had my song fallen on unhearing ears? I couldn't tell. I knew she needed time to absorb and interpret what she had heard.

"You are the same beautiful Nur," she said after a long silence. "But you are wiser. Thank you for your thoughts. I'm tired now. Leave me."

I left, feeling I had done the right thing, yet apprehensive, deeply apprehensive.

On my way back to our hut, I recalled Ariane and Preder lying side by side on their bellies. I became terrified. I prayed: Mother

Goddess, I know you were with me throughout this meeting. I know I'm whole, a person unto myself, but will being so spare my life? I'm so happy with Sedeth, but will I have the courage to fight for us to stay together?

Totally engrossed in recalling my meeting with the queen, I had forgotten about Lela's presence in our hut. She was in great pain as she considered the fate of her son. Her sobs grew stronger. I held her and made every effort to soothe her anguish. Our attention was drawn to her baby when he made loud gurgling sounds. We became absorbed by his beauty and quickly forgot our individual dilemmas, as the child immersed us in living and loving.

Sedeth reentered the hut and observed our joyful state, but ignored us. I noticed the dogged, terrified look in his eyes. He went to the far corner of the hut and busied himself with our evening meal. Lela left, cooing to her son.

Exhausted by my fears, I unexpectedly fell asleep. I awakened in the morning without Sedeth beside me and when I looked around, he was nowhere to be found. I called his name, thinking that he might have gone hunting.

I was five months pregnant, and though my slim body carried the child almost unnoticeably, its presence compelled me to adjust my customary pace. I couldn't bound off the ground as in earlier times, but needed the assistance of both hands and arms. I smiled to myself at how awkward I must look. But I didn't care, as long as the child inside my womb was happy and safe.

When I stepped outside the hut, I noticed that the women were assembling before the queen's quarters. Lela ran to me. Her slave, with the baby in his arms, was already at the meeting site. I wondered if Sedeth, too, was at the meeting, but he was nowhere to be seen. I asked the warrior women with whom he worked if they had noticed him at the stables. They had not seen him.

I looked around fearfully for him, wondering if he'd had another episode of terror and rage. Ill at ease, I stood beside Lela and her slave, waiting for the queen to make her entrance.

It was dramatic. She appeared before us clothed as a nonwarrior woman in a long, toga-like tunic, her right, singed breast covered, her left breast exposed. True to the custom of the Amazons, female children at the age of eight who aspired to become warriors for the *community had the flesh of their right breasts burned. The shriveled appendage made it easier to wield such weapons as the bow and arrow and ax during warfare. The Amazons were known to be an awesome sight on the battlefield, baffling many male warriors who fought against them. I appreciated the valor of our female warriors, but at this moment I was dumbstruck by the queen's manipulative display of femininity and her need to emphasize it by exposing her left breast. The intact breasts of nonwarrior women like Lela and me were always covered.*

Her long blond hair, usually gathered in a bun at the nape of her neck, was loose, falling in waves to the middle of her back. She wore soft hide boots on her feet; her hands carried no weapons. I couldn't believe her changed demeanor. My intuition caused me to feel a gathering dread.

Lela and all the nonwarrior women applauded when they saw her dressed in this way. Some shouted, "Hail the queen!"

The queen lifted her left arm, which represented the feminine side of her being, and waited for silence. In time the women gave their idol the silence she asked for and waited breathlessly for her verdict.

"I have been harsh. I can also be lenient. I do not wish to use harsh measures, but for our matriarchy to remain intact, harsh measures must sometimes be resorted to. I want you to understand that it is not easy to rule when we are surrounded by men who wish to annihilate us. We must procreate, therefore, and bring into our midst female children. It is not a question of using inhumane methods to eliminate male babies, but of ridding our community of a male population that could become our future downfall. That is why we use what seem to be cruel methods of elimination. I want to change this today.

"We know that Lela has given birth to a boy, who is now five months old. I leave the decision in your hands, women who are not warriors. Lela has grown to love her son. Yet if we make an exception, it may, in the long run, lead to our destruction."

The queen spied me in the crowd and a smile touched her lips, a smile that thanked me for my songs, which had given her these latest tools of propaganda. I was disgusted. My fears had been correct.

I watched the women into whose hands the decision had been placed. They were elated. The queen trusted them, considered them valuable. This consideration differed from the usual attitude toward nonwarriors, who, as a result of their unsinged breasts, were considered "ordinary women." Because of the honor bestowed on them now by the queen, they were determined not to betray her and the matriarchy. None of them wanted to hurt Lela, but there was a larger picture they had to consider—the welfare of their endangered community.

Ronald brushed the tears from my face tenderly. "Don't be afraid," he whispered.

You weren't around. Where were you? I asked silently.

The women huddled together for some time, Lela in the center. There was a great deal of arguing, until Lela, teary-eyed, emerged from the crowd and stood beside the queen.

In a broken voice, Lela said—according to the decision of the women—that she would relinquish her son to her slave, who would be free to return to his native land, where he must promise to raise the child devotedly.

The queen smiled a meager smile of approval, but I knew she was not pleased. She wanted death by acclamation for the male child. Furthermore, Lela's slave had too much information about our tribe, its location, its habits, and exactly where our warrior women were stationed on the perimeter of the community. Such information would be of inestimable value to the enemy.

Nevertheless, the queen continued her charade. I noticed her nod to the leader of the warrior women, who nodded back. I realized they had conspired beforehand. I concluded that, on the ordained day, the slave and the child would be killed at a safe distance from the community.

The queen announced that she would give Lela another night with the infant; then in the early morning the slave and their child would be freed, as decreed by the women. The women cheered the queen and hailed her as fair, with judgment that would henceforth never be questioned.

Lela held her infant close to her bosom. She returned to her hut with her slave. I knew she would not sleep but would watch over them both throughout the night, weeping.

I was weary, wearier than I had ever felt. I was grateful that I, a nonwarrior woman, abstained from making the decision along with the other nonwarrior women. I knew I would not have been able to control myself and would have endangered Sedeth's life, my baby's life, and my own life. Pondering on this grave matter, I suddenly wondered, Where is Sedeth? Where is he when I need him?

I walked slowly to our hut. When I was a few feet away, I saw a warrior woman on horseback outside it.

I ran to her, screaming, "What's wrong? Is it Sedeth? Where is he?"

She pointed toward the hut. I opened the flap. Lying on the mat on his belly, unconscious, was Sedeth, tied with his arms and legs behind him, as Ariane and Preder had been tied.

"He was running away from the community like a wild animal. He looked crazy. He didn't recognize me when I warned him to stop. I didn't kill him because I remembered him from the stables. I won't tell the queen. I know you can help him understand. I'll untie him, but if he runs away again, I can't guarantee I won't hurt him."

I thanked her profusely. After she left, I turned to him. "Sedeth, Sedeth, it's me, Nur. I'm here. You're safe. Everything is fine. Come back, Sedeth, my love. Come back."

I stroked his head. Such tenderness had brought him around before from his secret pain. He opened his eyes. When he saw me, he pulled me to him, holding me tightly, until he fell into a deep, exhausted sleep.

Beyond the point of exhaustion myself, beyond any weariness I might have ever felt previously, I fell asleep beside him.

When the man had been in trouble, I'd always shunned him for being weak. All attention should have been focused on me! Where had my lovingness gone? It was buried, misplaced. Dear God, what kind of woman have I become?

7
Sedeth Reveals Himself

"Nur, I mean Kendra! Wake up!" Ronald was shaking me. "Wake up. I've got to leave."

"You've just come back," I said, in a stupor. "Where were you? Why did you run away? Don't you think I need your help sometimes? Why are you always running away?"

"Kendra, Kendra," Ronald called out. "It's me, Ronald. I'm here. I have to leave because it's after six o'clock. They'll be waiting for me."

"Who'll be waiting for you?" I asked, still unable to focus on the present.

"My wife and others."

"I'm your wife, and I'm pregnant. You can't leave. We just found you."

"Kendra, snap out of it. Come back to the present. I'm *Ronald*, and I have to leave."

"I don't want you to leave!"

"For the time being, I have to. At least until things get clearer."

"I don't want you to leave. Stay next to me all night and hold me. That's the way it should be. You know it and I know it."

Ronald looked at his watch and groaned. "They'll be worried if I don't leave now."

"What about *me*?" I yelled.

"I can't help it. Be a big girl and let it evolve."

"No!" I shouted. "I'll be whoever I am!"

"Well, then, be whoever you are without me," he stated calmly.

I watched him put his shoes on and restrained my impulse to go to him. When he was finished, he went to the door, hoping I would come to him. But I didn't.

He disappeared into the night. I heard the sound of his car fade away as I stood by the door, dazed.

The phone rang. "Is Ronald on his way?" a female voice asked.

"Yes," I answered, my voice bland. "He's on his way. He left two minutes ago."

"Thank you," she said. We hung up.

"Thank you," I screamed at that disembodied voice. For what? For taking him away from me? For the fact that you exist—whoever you are? He's mine, not yours! I sobbed and sobbed. He's Sedeth and he's Ronald. They're both mine.

I went to bed weary. Nur had been weary, too.

We're both weary, I thought. I want to sleep hard, hard. In the morning I'll make sense out of all this. If I can't, I'll have to live through it, that's all.

The next morning the sun streamed through my windows as I blurrily opened one eye. Only partially awake, I yelled out into the air: "They're killing the child and the slave! They're killing the child and the slave!"

The phone rang. Ronald shouted over the phone, "The child is dead, and so is the slave!"

"How do you know that?" I cried, incredulously.

"How do you know what I'm talking about?" he countered.

"Because I know. We both know. The queen is evil. Oh, Ronald, I gave her the ideas she fooled the women with."

"What are you talking about?" he asked.

"I never told you, because you weren't there. You were too busy being terrified and running away. I didn't want to upset you, so I didn't tell you that I sang to her, and from my songs she got the idea of how to fool the nonwarrior women. She got the idea from Nur. Right now I'm so tired and so angry. All I want to do is yell, and then sleep. I've done the yelling. Now I'm hanging up!" And I did.

"So there!" I muttered in total exhaustion, as I fell into a dreamless sleep.

When I awakened again, the sun was at its height. I tried to get out of bed but couldn't. Just thirty little minutes more, I promised myself as I rolled over to my favorite side.

My next recollection was of someone calling my name. "Kendra, Kendra, you're still in bed?"

I opened my eyes to see Ronald standing there, taking off his clothes, then crawling under the sheets next to me.

"How did you get into my house?"

"You left the door open," he said, disappointed that I had not expected him.

"I must be losing it," I mumbled.

"Why are you still in bed?" he asked playfully.

"Because I'm tired and because I'm pregnant."

"Do you want me to hold you, pregnant woman?"

"I want you to hold me and devour me, even though I haven't washed, even though I haven't eaten, even though I'm angry at you."

"I'll do my best," Ronald promised.

"You will?" I asked challengingly. I didn't wait for him to act, however. I rolled on top of his body. "I'll show you what devouring is like." I started with his forehead and kissed every tiny section of his body down to the toes. They were loud, sometimes nipping, sometimes sloppy kisses.

He was bewildered, often reacting like a shy, ten-year-old boy. Throughout most of it, however, he giggled, gurgled, oohed, and aahed with pleasure.

"*That's* what I mean by devouring," I said, out of breath, satisfied with my demonstration.

"My God, Kendra! Who are you?"

"I'm Kendra," I replied nonchalantly. "And you are Ronald, and we're also Nur and Sedeth. We've known each other for centuries, but for reasons unknown to us, we haven't been able to consummate our passion since that Amazon life. Perhaps this is the first time we'll be able to attain some degree of consciousness about our connection. I think we should experience this connection to the end." I paused. "Come into the tub with me. I need to wash."

He agreed, and I put a heavily scented foam powder into the water. We lay in perfumed luxury at opposite ends of the whirlpool tub. Our pleasure was indescribable as we each peered through the bubbles at the other. When the bubbles rose between us, obscuring our sight of each other, we sprang toward the center of the tub and met there. We laughed and kissed and touched one another sensually.

Our energies blended. Once again we were transported to our hut, to a life lived seven thousand years ago—so long ago, yet just a wrinkle in time.

Sedeth awakened first, looking at me sheepishly. "I'm not much help to you, am I, Nur?"

I thought for a moment and told him with complete honesty that I, too, needed support in this difficult time. I said I expected him to be concerned about us, rather than with himself only. He nodded as though he understood. He looked at my swollen belly and asked how "she" felt inside.

I smiled warmly, telling him that "she" was warm, safe, and happy, but that her mother was very hungry. Neither of us had eaten since the previous day.

He brought food. As we ate, I described yesterday's event. When I mimicked the queen's portrayal of a nonwarrior woman, Sedeth laughed until his body hurt. He was surprised and excited to hear that the queen had put the fate of Lela's child into the women's hands. He grew downcast, however, upon hearing the decision Lela and the nonwarrior women had made about her slave and their infant.

"The queen will never let them go!" mourned Sedeth. "How can they be so naive? Have they left?"

"I believe they were scheduled to leave at sunrise. They're on their way," I explained, tears coming to my eyes. Sedeth buried his head in his hands.

"Treacherous woman," he roared, as though addressing the absent queen. "Infamous, treacherous woman! I loathe you! May your Mother Goddess punish you until you writhe in agony forever!"

He left the hut, unable to contain his anguish. I sat, immobilized.

"Must I always be alone with my pain?" I asked myself, returning to self-awareness. I became furious.

I went outside, a short distance from our hut, to find Sedeth pacing back and forth. He had to restrain his impulse to run, to fly, to shout, to go to the end of the earth and fall off its edge into nothingness. Only nothingness would relieve his anguish.

Without forethought, without caution, without care for his sensitive nature, I screamed at him. "I'm in need, too! I can't deal by myself with what is happening to us. Do you think you're the only one who feels anything? You're not! I'm also in pain! Lela is my friend. She must be in her hut alone, without her slave, without her beloved child—hoping, praying that he will somehow remember her when he grows up. But you know and I know that both of them are dead on the ground not far from here, slaughtered by the warrior women, slaughtered because it's a crime to bear a male child.

"There will not be a trace of them. Already the carcasses of the slave and the child have been thrown to the wild beasts, and soon the community will celebrate the beginning of a new regime, a regime in which the 'ordinary women' will have a voice."

I was stirred up almost to madness. I could not contain my feelings in my usual fashion. I sat on the ground, my hands wrapped around my belly, rocking the creation within my womb, wanting to protect it, to keep it safe from the queen's evil. I sobbed pitifully.

Sedeth watched me from a distance, knowing that any intervention from him would have been unwelcome.

When I was again in control, I looked in his direction. I hung my head as I recalled the heartfelt words I had sung to the treacherous queen.

"It was I, Sedeth, who gave her these ideas. It was I who sang to her of my feelings about what the community needed. I was the one who told her to be more womanly, that she was unbalanced without either a man in her life or a female energy within herself that was whole. It was I who had told her that life can't thrive with her fanatic hatred of men, that it must be lived from mercy, love, and wisdom. At that time I didn't know if she heard me. She was grateful and admiring, but that told me nothing. Little did I think she would misuse my message this way. Little did I think that she would be so devious."

I calmed down as my passion subsided. "She is not only devious but also fanatical beyond reason and can't be rescued. She adheres rigidly to her beliefs, because any beliefs other than her own terrify her. Yes, it's true that we Amazons had to liberate ourselves from male domination, but our own community should be guided by love, not deceit! Our nature must express balance! If we are as unbalanced as she is, as many of the women here are, there is no hope; there's only a disconnection from who we really are." The words I spoke came to me of their own accord, from another source inside me. "And who we really are is as large as the universe. This I know. This I will fight for and die for."

I didn't see Sedeth. I was focused on nothing except the emotions that were bursting forth from my heart. I'd been filled with these thoughts and feelings for a lifetime and at last they were being expressed.

Finally I caught a glimpse of Sedeth standing by a tree, enraptured by my passion, my honesty, my strength. I didn't need or want his approval. I rose from the ground and entered our hut to finish my meal.

I ate with enthusiasm for myself, for our child, for the three of us. I sang to the life inside me:

> *If you should see*
> *the light of day,*
> *my darling babe,*
> *oh, my darling,*
>
> *if you hear the birds*
> *singing in the trees,*
> *my darling babe,*
> *oh, my darling,*
>
> *then you will*
> *have been born.*
> *You will*
> *have been born.*
>
> *Live your life*
> *from your inner voice,*
> *my darling babe,*
> *oh, my darling.*
>
> *Your life will be blessed,*
> *my darling babe,*
> *oh, my darling.*
>
> *The angels' voices*
> *will guide you.*
> *They will guide you,*
> *to eternity.*

Sedeth came into our hut, sat before me on the mat, and listened to my song. He was silent. His eyes were gentle and kind; he had learned more about me.

"It's a lovely song, Nur." He hesitated, waiting to see if I was receptive. "You're a courageous woman. I admire and envy your conviction, your strength, and your connection to yourself. In contrast, I feel so powerless. I can see I'm not a balanced man."

He paused, thinking, then continued: "It's partly because I'm a male at the mercy of a community of women in which I'm unable to express my male strength. My male self—it has expression only with you, my love." Sedeth paused again, then said softly, "But also, that imbalance is partly because I'm burdened with a past that almost drowns me.

"I've never told you this, but when I was a little boy, I saw my father, a nobleman, hacked to death by his best friend. I was the only witness to his crime. Had I not fled, I would have met the same fate. I ran to my mother and told her the murderer's name. She was grief-stricken and, at the same time, terrified for my safety. 'You must go away from here,' she told me. From the time I was five, she made sure I was shuttled from one place to another. She paid a heavy price to those who sheltered me. I never found out why that man killed my father, but his anger was so great that he wanted to do away with all traces of my father's lineage. The murderer continued to menace me, however.

"I seldom saw my mother. My loveless life was lived in different homes. I could never become a part of a household. Sooner or later I was targeted by my father's killer, quickly uprooted by those who cared for me, and sent elsewhere. My education was erratic, my sense of belonging nonexistent.

"I despise injustice, Nur. This hatred lives in my entrails like a monster ready to spring, but when I'm face-to-face with it, I freeze in terror. I become crazed and paralyzed. I think seeing such a brutal crime at a young age contorted my brain. I can do nothing other than flee. I have no control over myself." He added softly, "I pray this will change."

Sedeth looked at me, hoping I would not be disgusted by him. When he felt my assurance he continued.

"It was when I ran from my last home that your queen captured me. Her warrior women were pillaging the village where I lived. I watched them ransack the homes and kill the villagers. I could have escaped, but instead my body froze. I fell to the ground, where the women warriors bound me and placed me on a horse to be brought here.

"*The only good thing about this place is that I met you, Nur—you, the woman I love and will always love. I hope I never disappoint you.*"

I put my hands on his face, my forehead against his. I felt clearer about him and had a better understanding of the rage and terror that sometimes overcame him. I intoned silently: Meet my strength, my love. Meet my strength.

We broke our embrace only when Lela came into our hut. She was elated. She'd had a vision of her little son calling to her, telling her he would never forget her.

Sedeth and I felt great sorrow, for we knew a truth that Lela did not. We cried together with the woman who had been blessed by a vision that gave her hope.

8
A Depth in All of Us

I gave Ronald a towel to dry himself. When I noticed the bubbles from the bathwater still on his body, I rubbed his skin until they disappeared. He then dried my body from head to foot and led me back to my bed.

We sat against the headboard of my queen-size bed, leaning on two fluffy pillows. He held my right leg in his lap, massaging it, pulling my toes, which cracked willingly under his touch. It felt so good that I changed position, placing my other leg in his lap for him to do the same.

While massaging my leg, he said, to my surprise, "You know there's a similarity between Sedeth's life and mine. I was also shuffled from one foster home to another after the age of five. My mom couldn't take care of me. She had divorced my father, who was never at home anyway. I hardly remember him.

"In five years, I was in three different foster homes. No one wanted to keep me. They said I was too rambunctious." Ronald's mouth twisted. "My feeling is," he said, obviously disgusted, "they wanted a dog that they could train instead of a child they had to pay attention to. But I learned to adjust to some of my foster parents' needs so I wouldn't starve. I remember in one situation, the couple who was keeping me were former European aristocrats who had lost their wealth in the political upheaval of their native country. They had been forced to emigrate to the United States. They denied me food until I learned to eat the peas on my fork by biting into them instead of using my lips to pull them into my mouth. They insisted on making me into an aristocratic son, as rigid as they were.

"Do you want to see what it looks like to eat peas on a fork without using your lips?" Ronald digressed playfully. "It's the only way I can eat them to this day. Watch."

He pantomimed the action, puckering up his lips, then biting into the peas so they would enter his mouth. When they were in his mouth, he bit into each one of them with his teeth, except for one that kept falling out of his mouth. He pursued the fallen pea, attempting to pick it up with his teeth, still not using his lips.

He was on the floor chasing the tiny rolling green tidbit while I watched him from the bed, convulsed with laughter.

"What's wrong with using your lips?" I asked.

"It's *common*," Ronald replied with a laugh. "Only common people use their lips when they eat. Aristocrats bite into their food with their teeth."

"How did they kiss?"

"I've already figured that one out," he answered. "Like this."

He leaped from the floor to the bed and, before I could stop him, gave me an aristocratic kiss.

"Ouch," I cried. "That hurts."

"I guess that's why they didn't do much kissing," Ronald grinned mischievously. "I can't remember ever seeing them kiss, not even their own two small sons.

"At ten, my birth mother remarried and I found myself in a permanent home with a stepfather. He and I didn't get along. I was miserable. They tell the story of my running away every day during summer vacation. They finally found me sitting on the lawn of a house I had selected as my true home. I remember that I sat there every day for what seemed like hours, like a Buddha, with my eyes closed, singing to myself. I wanted that family to look out their windows, see me, and adopt me. I did this for weeks, until my mom followed me and brought me back to our house.

"It was anything but a loving family life. I never had one. I left as soon as I could. I married at an early age, but that was a mistake. When I met my present wife, I divorced the first one." Ronald fluffed up his pillow, turned to me, and asked, "What about your life?"

"I've been married, but it didn't work out. After I divorced I had other relationships, which also didn't work out. So I stopped all romantic relating and began to probe my problems about men. Now I've met you and I'm ready to go forward. Are you?"

Instead of answering, Ronald focused his attention on how I was holding my head while I talked. "Loosen up," he advised, massaging my neck so I would feel a better connection to my head.

"What's wrong with how I hold it?"

"You're tilting it back slightly," he responded. "Notice how you feel when it's not tilted."

I concentrated on the position of my head and neck after his massage. I found my head better connected, sitting straighter on my neck. As a result, I perceived reality somewhat differently. "I feel different," I remarked, still adjusting my head. "It's as though I see things more clearly."

"Really?" he asked. "Like what?"

"Like you. You just avoided my question about whether or not you're ready to go forward."

"You're right," he acknowledged. "The fact is that I don't know where I'm going. My wife and I were happy together for fourteen years. We've gone through a lot together, yet in the last year, she's grown increasingly critical of me as I've become more assertive. She's a strong woman.

"I'm tired of not being my own person, my own man. I've been subjugated by women since I was born, and I want a change. The more independent I become, the more threatened my wife feels. Her reaction to my independence is always criticism, irritability, making herself into an indomitable monarch. It's disturbing the equilibrium of the whole marriage. She and I haven't had sex for a year. We just talk endlessly, trying to straighten out our differences. In the meantime, I've become deeply attracted to you and want to be with you all the time."

Ronald paused, then summed up. "Kendra, I don't know if I'm ready to go forward."

I pulled my head and neck away from his grasp. "What are we doing then? What am I doing with you?"

"We can't help ourselves," he burst out.

"Phooey!" I responded. Once again I consciously placed my head in an upright position on my neck, giving myself greater mental clarity.

"You only want to play. To me, relating is not a game. Like Sedeth, you've had an unsettled life. And even though you've been married for years, I'm sure you've been unfaithful to your wife. Haven't you? Be honest, Ronald."

"Yes," he replied, looking at me with apprehension. "I did have some affairs, but I found they weren't the answer to the restlessness inside me."

"What is the answer?"

"To be my own man, my own person. I married my wife because she's strong and, in many ways, takes better care of me than my mom did. It's not all one-sided, though. I give her a lot, too. We've grown during the time we've been together. But I've become like her slave, which makes her feel like a queen. She takes her role as a queen way too seriously, and when I won't surrender to her every desire, her impulse is to annihilate me.

"God, Kendra, you're making me think of things that have been stuck inside me, things I don't really want to look at. But all this introspection makes me realize that I've got a lot to sort out. Can't we just take a few minutes to cuddle? Let me massage you, which is what I'm here to do anyway. How about it?"

Ronald's eyes pleaded with me to let him rest. "All right," I smiled with compassion. "Hold me tight, tighter than ever, and let's breathe together."

"It feels so good to hold you. We're both starved for affection. It feels so good." Ronald put his leg across my body and brought me closer to him.

"It does," I crooned. "It feels so good and so right."

He kissed me deeply while his hands caressed my body. I felt wanted, desired. The effects of my years of celibacy were being healed; my body was becoming alive, my womanliness reviving.

"You smell good, taste good, and you are good—maybe too good for me," he whispered, immersed in his passion.

"Maybe."

"Don't spoil it," he said, somewhat peeved.

"Then don't feed me your doubts."

"You're right. Let's both shut up and breathe ourselves back into our other life. I no longer feel like Ronald. I'm becoming handsome, blond, much younger—and oh, so sexually potent."

"I feel younger, too. Dark skinned, filled with your child. I'm a special young woman."

Our wills blended to become one. The sound of the waterfall came and went quickly.

"You're a special young woman," said Sedeth. He returned to my side after letting Lela out of the hut. Suddenly he exclaimed, "Look at your belly, Nur! It's getting bigger every day. I love touching it." We laughed as we noticed the life inside shifting around.

"Oh, my dearest Nur, perhaps you're right to go to the queen to tell her about our child. Let her know we wish to remain together. Plead with her, remind her of her love for your mother. Tell her again how important it is to be balanced. Remind her that the community can't withstand another horrible deed perpetrated for the sake of matriarchal beliefs.

"Tell her we would be willing to leave the community and fend for ourselves. Tell her in the name of your mother and her long devotion to the queen that you would never divulge the secrets of the community. Make her believe you! She can't betray her love for you! She can't betray the loyalty of your dead mother!

"Do this, my Nur," he went on rapidly. "Perhaps we'll have a chance to live out our lives. Tell her she's proven she can be a male-energized woman. Challenge her to be as feminine as her male energy is male."

I was dumbfounded by Sedeth's changed attitude, but delighted as well. "My precious love, I'm happy you've come around and want her to know."

"I feel this way because the not knowing feeds the crazed part of me. I no longer want to let myself get into such a state. I can't go to her myself. She wouldn't give an audience to a slave unless you brought me."

"Preder accompanied Ariane," I said. "I don't know how active the queen allowed him to be in her presence. But I know you to be an impressive speaker. We'll go together, although I'll first have an audience with her privately. She'll feel more respected if we do it that way.

"She's always been interested in nonwarrior women's problems. I believe she'll welcome hearing about mine, particularly since I've seldom confided in her," I told him, optimism brightening my eyes. "I'll go to her as soon as she invites me to her quarters. Thank you, Sedeth, for making it so easy this time."

"In the country of my birth, I learned to pray to the gods when there was difficulty," Sedeth said softly, his arms around me as I leaned back against his strong chest, his hands on my round belly. "I learned to speak to stronger forces outside of myself; and sometimes I felt I was being helped. I'm aware that in this community you call on a deity, a female goddess. I should like to sit in silence with you, my love, and call on our various deities, invoking their help so we can have a successful meeting with the queen. Perhaps we'll be able to fulfill our lives with one another and have peace."

We left our hut and sat side by side on the bank of our stream, our eyes closed, calling upon the deities we were familiar with. We asked fervently for their help in what we both knew was a life-and-death struggle.

My heart became heavy as I tuned into the heartbeat of the life inside my womb and she spoke to me. I heard her voice telling me she was female. She spoke to me of our meeting each other in a place where life was balanced and joy boundless. I was disturbed by what I heard, but kept it a secret from Sedeth. I hoped such thoughts were the products of my fanciful imagination.

After a while Sedeth moved from his position to sit behind me. He held my breasts and my abdomen. As the sun sank slowly, we became purified in its gentle radiance. I willed it to burn into every crevice of my body as well as my baby's body, igniting in me my own fire, my own power and vastness. I was aglow.

Sedeth then lifted me up from the ground and carried me into our hut. Throughout the night he was more tender and sensitive than ever before.

I slept in his arms, grateful for the life we shared. I thought, If this is our last peaceful sleep, let me remember how it has been. Let me not forget the fullness and richness of our togetherness.

Within two days, I was called to the queen's hut. As I approached it, I remembered that I, along with the other nonwarrior women, had always been impressed by the queen's simplicity in living. Her hut was no more elaborate than Sedeth's and mine. She had the help of two warrior women who cooked for her and served her meals, who attended to her clothes and maintained the condition of her quarters. But otherwise, the queen had always insisted that she live no differently from any of the other women in her community. She earned great respect from the matriarchy for her liberal attitude.

When I approached the entrance, she was standing by the door, her arms extended to embrace me. I returned her embrace, feeling her love for me. She suddenly pushed me away from her to scan my body and rested her eyes on my abdomen. She smiled happily until I told her in a businesslike manner that I wanted to speak of issues other than the pregnancy.

"Oh, of course." Rage flickered briefly in her eyes, but in the next moment she expertly pushed back her feelings and referred to my mother. "She would have been proud of you. She was such a beautiful woman—elegant, gracious, poised like you, Nur."

She led me inside the hut, to the largest mat on the ground. As she did so, I looked around, remembering when I was a child how often she had placed a smaller mat next to hers and urged me to spend the night with her, particularly after my mother's death. She would reach over from her mat and hold my hand, telling me she loved me and would take care of me forever. I would smile happily, at the same time pushing away the longing for my beloved mother.

I looked into the corner of the hut where the queen kept her numerous saddles and weapons. Her only luxury was a wooden tub in which she bathed instead of cleansing her body in the stream, as did the rest of the community. A smile came across my lips as I recalled playing in the tub, standing, legs apart, left arm extended, pretending I was the great queen.

I couldn't help chuckling to myself. I muffled it, however, as I sat down on the mat facing her.

She began to reminisce about her friend:

"I will never forget your mother's contributions to the community. She helped in the education of both the children and the women, making herself available to all of us with a generosity and kindness that was unmatched. What a beautiful nature!"

I lowered my head, partially out of embarrassment, partially from guilt about my reasons for being there. Were my mother alive, I mused, I would right now have the security of her love and her wisdom, instead of the gnawing fear that Sedeth and I live in most of the time.

My introspection made the queen unsure of the clarity of my attention. She fidgeted for a while, not knowing what to do, until once again she looked at my full body. She then burst into pleased laughter; it was contagious and restored harmony to our conversation.

The queen was now at ease and told me, as though she were confessing it: "I could never understand why your mother did not abhor her monstrous husband. Yet, she never spoke unkindly about him and only expressed compassion for his ignorance. You, too, have little vengeance in your heart for men, who look upon women as inferior beings. In fact, you have little vengeance in your heart for anyone. What are you made of that causes you and your mother to be so different from the rest of us?" She turned away, as though hoping to find an answer in her own nature. I knew she had no inkling about the diligent work self-transformation entailed.

My heart pounded as I waited for her to turn again and face me. When she did, I finally found the courage to answer her. "My nature tells me to look upon everyone with love, my queen, as I do you and those in the matriarchy. I look upon Sedeth with love—as a beautiful specimen of man. If you want to know how it's done, I probe his nature to find his beauty. I've done that, and I've found the core of his beauty and strength. I've discovered I would be happy to remain with it for the rest of our lives.

"There is depth in all of us. To discover that depth in another human being, one must be willing to dig patiently into that being's soul. Had my mother not been willing to do this with my father, she would have perceived him only as a monster who deserved merciless punishment. Yet I don't recall in our ten years together ever hearing her disparage him. Instead, she spoke of his inner beauty and kindness. She also spoke of his ignorance, taught to him by a society that believed male energy was so much greater than female energy.

"My mother knew that his ignorance was created by his unwillingness to recognize what his heart told him. Instead, he blindly accepted male superiority. My mother felt that anyone who ignores the balance of the female and male energies in himself or herself is miserably ignorant."

I paused, taking her hand in mine, then continued: "She loved you, my queen, and wished to make you aware of your feminine beauty. That's why you loved her. She wasn't condemning of your lopsidedness. She was encouraging you to be more than you are, to bring out your creative, feminine, tender qualities so you would have balance. Only when we are balanced will we be whole. When we're whole, we join the universe."

The queen listened, enraptured. Her soul was hungry for this kind of truth. My mother and I had always been examples to her of such truth. But the queen was too fearful to experience it for herself. She gently disengaged her hand from mine, placing both of her hands on the mat, her head away from me. She continued to listen intently.

"As a matriarchy," I went on, "our community can continue to defend the freedom of women, but within our community grant us freedom to look for that balance. Be true to your feminine nature as well as to your male, warrior nature. Do not betray that male nature, but do not ignore the feminine side of yourself, either. Give Sedeth permission to attend our next meeting. Allow him to speak. You'll see a male nature looking for balance, striving for it."

Now I took the plunge. "We want to wed. If it can't happen in our community, then free us to fend for ourselves. I would make a vow not to divulge anything about our matriarchy, a vow as sacred as my love for my mother."

I was excited. I was breathless. I spoke with a passion that clearly made the queen uneasy. Her gaze remained focused on the mat on which she sat.

"What do you want from me, Nur?" she asked, without looking up.

"I know you can be merciful. My mother knew this about you as well. Let Sedeth come to our next meeting, as I have requested. Remember that I love you and will always be grateful for your guardianship."

The queen kept her eyes on her mat; her fingernails dug into it. She was quiet for a long time. Since she said nothing, I rose and headed for the door. "Thank you," I told her with heartfelt sincerity, "for seeing me."

"Nur," she called, but again dropped her head. There was a silence, a silence I didn't understand. I walked slowly out of her hut, and even more slowly to the stream near where Sedeth and I lived.

I sat and wept tears of elation and exhaustion. A stabbing, grabbing, sinking feeling had filled my body. I realized that the commotion in my gut was the unspoken fury I had absorbed from the queen.

That, then, was the nature of her silence. I myself was devoid of fury: speaking the truth brings relief, not rage. I had fought for our lives.

The next move was in her hands.

I don't trust women. They want to mold you according to their image. God help you if you want something different from them. It's always been like that. I never spoke up—too afraid. Nur does. Let me learn from you, Nur. That courage was in me then.

If You Hear the Birds—

In spite of the queen's silence on parting, the next day Sedeth and I were summoned to her hut. I was fearful but in control. I noticed that Sedeth's body had stiffened radically.

He took my hand as we walked through the matriarchal hamlet filled with tents and huts. We greeted a few nonwarrior women, chatted with them casually. They smiled on seeing my expanding abdomen and asked how long it would be before the birth. We answered their questions graciously and moved on to the queen's quarters. I absorbed their good feelings toward us, which gave me confidence. I squeezed Sedeth's hand; he squeezed mine. We braced ourselves for what was to come.

As we entered the hut, the queen rose from her mat, greeted me in her usual manner, then turned her full attention to Sedeth. She faced him directly and scanned his entire body from his feet to his head. As she noticed his blond hair and blue eyes, features similar to hers, she smiled warmly at him.

She beckoned us both to sit on the mats in front of her.

I had noticed on entering that she was dressed in nonwarrior clothing, with both her left breast and her singed right breast covered. Her long blond hair flowed loosely down her back. I was perplexed by the way she was dressed. The only time I had seen her in such apparel was when the nonwarrior women met to deal with Lela's case. The queen ignored me, giving all her attention to Sedeth, who seemed to be relaxing in it. She offered us an intoxicating drink that had been made ready by her warrior women servants. Sedeth gulped it down. I sipped it slowly. As the time passed, the queen became increasingly coquettish with Sedeth. He, for no other reason than to free himself from his maddening terror, responded flirtatiously. When the queen noticed his response, I could tell she felt victorious.

The interrogation began. The queen carried it out with the utmost delicacy and with intimations of interest in our welfare. She asked Sedeth directly: *"You would like to marry Nur and remain in the community?"*

"Yes," Sedeth replied.

The queen offered us more food and drink, which had been set on a mat near us, then smiled enticingly at him. *"Do you also believe in the balance of the male and female energies in our natures, as does Nur?"* she asked with great interest.

"I do," he replied, *"but I must confess I'm not so well organized with my male nature as I should be. Nur is helping me develop that part of myself."* He looked at me gratefully.

"I suppose you feel I have an overabundance of male energy and am lacking in female energy," the queen sighed.

Sedeth, captivated by her willful charm and also intoxicated by drink, answered her in the way he knew she wanted to be answered. *"Many might learn from your male energy. And your female energy must be . . . shall I say, encouraged?"*

The queen was charmed, looking deeply into his eyes. Sedeth invited her gaze, which encouraged her even more to make an utter spectacle of herself.

"Nur thinks I am a deficient female, don't you, Nur?" She turned her back on me, not waiting for my response, and offered Sedeth more to drink.

I sat as though alone, watching them indulge one another. Whenever the queen acknowledged my presence, she did so with disdain. I couldn't help but think she was proving me wrong about her lack of female power by seducing my beloved. And to my chagrin, she was succeeding. I felt humiliated, defeated, and left out.

There was no discussion of our future. It was a masterful manipulation on her part. When we left, Sedeth actually kissed her cheeks. She delighted in the intimacy. She hardly bade me farewell.

I was silent on the way to our hut, making every conceivable effort to decipher the queen's mysterious and absurd behavior. And what of Sedeth? I rationalized that his terror made him lose perspective on reality, resulting in his betrayal of me, his love. He didn't understand that her behavior had been a subterfuge. What aim was she concealing? What kind of scheme was she perpetrating?

That night, Sedeth slept peacefully while I stayed awake almost until morning. I reasoned for the hundredth time that by seducing my love, the queen had succeeded in convincing herself that she was feminine and I was wrong. Sedeth had unintentionally colluded with her. Under such circumstances why would she believe herself to be without feminine qualities, to be an unbalanced woman? If she believed she was balanced, she would have no need to admire or emulate either my mother or me. She all but canonized my mother, both while she was alive and since her death. Our meeting had surely convinced the queen that my mother and I were no longer role models she needed to emulate. The two of us were now dispensable. Mother was dead, therefore I was the one who was dispensable. But how would she dispense with me? I asked myself, feeling a chill go through my body.

When morning came, hoping for some relief from my deep confusion about the queen's motives, I walked to the stream. Inwardly I was frantic. I needed to cleanse my body, purify it, protect the life within me.

I bathed in the water and washed the impurities from yesterday's meeting off my body. I instantly felt like myself again, felt my baby within me. I lay at the stream's edge, my feet in the cool water, looking at the sky, the blue cloudless sky. I recalled the words I had sung before to my baby, my beautiful baby inside my womb:

> If you should see
> the light of day,
> my darling babe,
> oh, my darling,
>
> If you hear the birds
> singing in the trees,
> my darling babe,
> oh, my darling,
>
> Then you will
> have been born.
> You will
> have been born.

A chill came into the air and into my flesh. It felt eerie. I became afraid. Even the sky above seemed to have darkened.

From the corner of my eye I saw shadows moving in the bushes. Screams broke out from my throat before I was aware of them. "Sedeth! Sedeth! By the stream! I need you!"

I saw him running toward me at the same time two warrior women leapt out of the bushes. One grabbed my arms, the other my legs. They pulled me to our hut, my back scraping along the earth. I screamed with pain. Sedeth ran after us into the hut. He tried to pull them away from me. Brutally they pushed him into a corner, where he cowered, rigid with terror. He opened his mouth, but nothing came forth. He was paralyzed . . . once again a child, a five-year-old, witnessing the murder of his protector.

The warrior woman holding my legs spread them far apart and pitilessly inserted a long stick into my womb. The pain made my eyes bulge, contorting my face and body.

I screamed. "No! No! No! Not my child! Why? Why? Treacherous woman! You cannot have my child!"

I twisted and turned my body from one side to the other to push them away from me, but the damage had been done. I felt the warm blood oozing from inside me. I lay in my blood and the blood of my child. The ground became saturated in it.

Slowly I fell toward unconsciousness. My eyes searched for Sedeth in the corner of the hut. Dimly I saw the man I loved, frozen, his mouth open, staring blindly at my dying body.

The women left, not realizing they had killed me. The queen's instructions, I was certain, were to mutilate my womanhood. She had planned to put my femininity on the same level with hers. She had succeeded better than she planned—it was dead.

Sedeth's arms kept reaching ineffectually toward my body. He was mute, incapable of uttering a sound. Gradually his immobilized body thawed from its rigidity. He crawled toward me and dropped one ear to my chest to listen for my heartbeat, but by that time my heart had stopped. He shook my body, hoping to revive me. He was soaked in my blood. His mouth was open: moans, groans, squeals emerging at last from his cramped throat. He embraced my body, trying to bring warmth to it. I was lifeless. He panted so forcefully that at last a shriek broke through from within him. The shriek became louder, until he was yelling my name: "Nur! Nur! Come back! Don't leave me! I need you!" Then he lost consciousness.

The queen was told of the warrior women's blunder. She came to our hut immediately on horseback. The sight that greeted her, and the memory of my mother, brought terrible remorse and tears to her eyes. What have I done? she asked herself. I wanted to teach you a lesson, Nur. I didn't want to kill you. You were presumptuous. I am your queen, and I was good to you. I only wanted to teach you a lesson. She gave the warrior women instructions to bury my body and bring Sedeth to her hut.

There, she attended to him personally, cleaning his unconscious body, washing away my blood. She massaged him with oils. In time he awakened, calling my name, "Nur! Nur! Where are you?"

"Nur is gone, Sedeth. Nur is gone," the queen said gravely. Sedeth wept for many days. His anguish was endless. "Nur come back! Please come back!"

Ronald clutched my body. I was motionless. "Nur! Kendra! Come to life. Don't play games!" Ronald pleaded, poking me. "You're awake now, aren't you? You're alive, aren't you? I love you! I can't live without you. Nur, Kendra, open your eyes. I love you! I can't live without you. Nur, Kendra, open your eyes!"

I was almost comatose, so deeply was I involved with the tragedy from the other life. I slithered up from my unconscious state to find Ronald staring into my face, sobbing uncontrollably.

"Oh, Kendra, how I loved you. How stupid I was. It was because of my stupid, thick ego that you were killed. Oh, Kendra, I want to learn from this experience. I'll never be the same."

"Nor will I," I said sluggishly, when I could find my voice. "There's a lot to sort out. Let's spend the night together and work on it. I know it's after six o'clock, but you can't leave me in this state and go home to the queen. You just can't do that."

"I've got to—until I'm clearer." Ronald was wretched.

I got to my feet unsteadily. "You know something? You'll never be clearer, because you don't want to be. So go—go to your mommy queen. Go and don't come back. I'll figure it out by myself, as I've always done. As Nur did. What will you be doing with the queen? Making nice? Go, Ronald, before I hate you forever."

He froze. I looked at his immobilized body. I pushed him out the bedroom door and locked it. I returned to bed, where I sobbed hysterically.

Alone, always alone. Is this Your design for me, God? Do I have to prove for the rest of my life that I can be strong? I'm angry with all of you—with you, Ronald; you, queen; You, God! What do You expect from me? What kind of superhuman strength are you all expecting? Well, I'm not superhuman. I'm human, and that's all I want to be. And I want to be met by someone who is also human.

"But, at the same time, I don't want to be cruel to Ronald, the way I just was. Help me remain compassionate—devoid of tyranny."

You didn't kill me, Mother, like the queen did, but you wanted to. And you, Father, you betrayed me. You acknowledged her evil and pushed me aside.

10
Sedeth's Story

I returned to my bed. It was in disarray from Ronald's presence. I sensed him everywhere. I longed for him but willfully dismissed the feeling.

If you call, Ronald, I thought, I won't answer the phone this time. Figure out your life for yourself. I'm not going to support you and serve you as Nur did. Most likely your sensitive, overdeveloped female nature evokes from women their need to mother a man. I won't fall into that trap. I'm not taking care of you! Taking care of you . . . Why does the phrase "taking care of you" come to my mind repeatedly?

I was emotionally and physically exhausted, even though I hadn't left my bed for the previous twenty-four hours. I rested my head on the pillows and, breathing slowly and deeply, massaged my higher energy centers, those at the heart, third eye, and crown. I had discovered that when the body breathes fully and these centers are open, one's imaging ability becomes available. I hoped to communicate with my own higher self, the consciousness of Nur, which I knew existed in another realm even as it also existed in me. With patience and quiet receptivity, I sought to contact Nur, to converse with this special being who could give me insights into this seemingly chaotic existence of mine.

No sooner had these energy centers become alive than I envisioned the image of a door sliding open, quietly, gently, until I saw a vast panorama ahead of me. I fused with the vastness, becoming one with the clouds, the blue sky, and with shapes that became more and more distinct. The shapes drifted in my direction until a particular presence beckoned to me. It seemed very familiar.

I recognized Nur's beautiful quality in my body and sensed her energy surrounding me. Her presence felt like a golden halo. Her radiant emanations poured through me. I was in touch with the consciousness of Nur.

Awestruck, I finally addressed her. "There you are, beautiful, kind, sensitive Nur. They killed you. What a horrible death. I feel the pain of their butchery in my own body. I wonder if that trauma, seven thousand years old, is still lodged in my womb as memory scars, affecting my life today? I believe it is so. I believe I've responded in this life to those scars in an unconscious way, as an irrational fear of pregnancy and as an irrational fear of surrendering to a man, as well as a perpetual fear of betrayal.

"Your soul is my soul, sweet Nur. As you were dying you watched Sedeth cowering in the corner of the hut. You also witnessed the queen's regret at her evil deed. What were you feeling and thinking? What happened to Sedeth after your death? Let me bring your energy through me and let me fuse with you. Help me get answers to the puzzle that is me, answers that will help me understand the energy between Ronald and me, between all men and me."

"...between Ronald and me, between all men and me." These last words I spoke to Nur suddenly grabbed hold of my psyche until the deep pain I felt about my confusion regarding men turned into unrestrained sobs.

"Oh, Nur, I'm sorry, so sorry," I cried helplessly. "I'm so bereft, so anxious to be clearer. Until that happens, I'll feel lost and hopeless." Nur's energy enveloped my body and I was nurtured by the comfort she gave me.

"*You have many questions, Kendra. They can't all be answered at once. I sympathize with your deep need to understand and rectify. Insights into yourself will become available to you. All will evolve. Be patient, my love.*"

"Forgive me, Nur, for my ravenous need. When I get disappointed in someone's behavior, as I did with Ronald's, once again I feel as though the mountains weep with me. So bottomless is the depth of my pain, I become swallowed up in it."

"*How well I understand your pain, Kendra, and sympathize with it. Your pain is my pain.*"

"Thanks. I'm all right now. I guess I needed your understanding and sympathy." I wiped away my tears and leaned against my headboard. "What happened to Sedeth?"

"Sedeth is taken care of by the queen. His anguished mourning resounds to the heavens, so that again and again I'm pulled back to earth to help him. In time, however, his grief lessens as the business of daily living occupies him. At the queen's request, he remains in her quarters. He's free to come and go as he pleases if he's not occupied in the stables. When the day's chores are finished, Sedeth goes to our stream, where he cleanses himself, lies on the bank, and calls to me.

"I appear to him in spirit form, stroking his forehead, singing our love song in his ears. He recalls our love for one another and reaches his arms and hands into the air, wanting to touch me. His longing is momentarily satisfied, but in time he finds our contact too ephemeral. He shouts angrily that I should not have left him, that I should have been less outspoken with the queen. Had I been more diplomatic, he says, she would have given us what we wanted. Why was it not clear to me on the afternoon of our meeting that he was succeeding in winning her over? Wasn't it apparent that she would have given him whatever he demanded?

"I become angered by his lack of reality and by his need to twist the truth into a lie to assuage his conscience. I portray graphically in the ether the moment of my butchery and his frozeness in the corner of the hut. I forcefully imprint the horror of this scene into the atmosphere, so its reality is unmistakable. Sedeth runs from my depiction and from me. I am relentless in my anger and follow him into the stream. I follow him when he runs into the woods. I follow him into the stables. I follow him everywhere until he begs me to stop. I withdraw. He no longer calls for me."

"I'm glad you were so forceful, Nur," I said out loud. "You were too kind to him, too loving, too understanding."

"Such was my nature at that time. Can one be different when one loves unconditionally? I've learned since then never to bestow godship on a man."

"How much undoing of karmic misdeeds that must entail," I sighed despondently. "Will I ever be that loving again?" A sense of hopelessness surged through me, but I fought it off. After a while, I asked, "What happened to Sedeth after he stopped contacting you?"

"He established a pattern with women that's haunted him all of his life. He avoided being reminded of the truth of our unhappy ending. From time to time I would hear my name being called in the atmosphere, but it would evaporate before it reached my soul."

"Are you still angry at him?"

"*Compassion is the truer feeling I have now.*"

"I hope I can feel that way with Ronald," I told her, praying that my nature would change. "What happened then?"

"*I see it as though it were happening now. The queen is drawn to him as to a son. She gives him constant attention, cooking for him, truly concerned about his welfare. She confides in Sedeth about the problems of ministering to the community. He listens attentively, all the while scheming to make her totally dependent on him. It's a long story, Kendra. Are you sure you want to hear all the details?*"

"All of them," I said, hungry to understand myself more, as well as Ronald.

"All right," continued Nur. "*The effect of their daily closeness awakens the queen's female self. She begins to look at him longingly, becoming more coquettish and petulant at Sedeth's lack of response. 'Is it the difference in our ages?' asks the queen. 'Do you need more time to forget Nur? Do you not find me appealing? Tell me what you want and it will be yours.' She's obsessed with him.*

"*One evening she gives him the same intoxicating drink as she did at the time of our fatal meeting. Sedeth succumbs to her sexual advances. He caresses her hard, muscular body with its singed breast, barely able to fend off her sexual ferocity. He feels he's engaged in warfare. She clutches his sexual organ savagely, until it becomes flaccid. Her rage toward men is revealed by her aggressive manipulation of his body. Her energy is released in ways other than sexual intercourse: she bites, scratches, pummels, and pounces on her traumatized lover.*

"*Finally satiated, she lies by Sedeth's side. He wishes to vomit and flee. She demands that he hold her throughout the night as he had held me. 'As I held Nur!' is his thought, tears coming to his eyes.*

"*In the morning he awakens to the grotesque woman warrior by his side. He pushes himself away from her and leaves the hut. He runs to the stream, where he cleanses his body of the queen's odor. 'Nur, Nur,' he calls, 'you were right. She wanted to get rid of you so she could have me and prove she's a woman. Nur, she's not a woman. She's a bedeviled beast. I must get away from her. I must find a way to leave this place.'*

"*I feel bitter that it took him this long to wake up. I don't answer him. I decide that he must find his own way. He returns to the hut to find her standing with her arms open, expecting to be embraced.*

The queen is in love. After her sexual experience with Sedeth, she feels more than ever that I was wrong about her."

"I feel nauseous, Nur," I interrupted.

"I understand what you mean, Kendra, but such are the results of compromise. Do you want to go on?"

"Yes," I tell her, making a disgusted face.

"This is not too easy for me either. Recalling his tragedy makes me sad. I wish I had been wiser. But I've learned since then that unconsciousness is like an unwieldy ox. It has to be prodded forcefully to change its patterns."

"It's a good point, Nur. I've often wanted to kick myself after creating a messy mistake. Wow! What a story!"

"We all have monumental stories to tell about our lives. The important thing is to look for them and change them. Let's go on.

"Sedeth accepts her embrace and kisses her lightly on the cheeks. He smiles. 'Do you remember you wanted to give me anything I desired?' She smiles back. 'Yes, I remember. What would you like?' she asks, as though about to bestow her kingdom upon him.

"'I would like a horse, a white one, the one you ride when you go to battle. I haven't had a horse of my own since I was a young boy. I'd like to ride around the territory of the community to make certain it's properly protected. I'd like to have more responsibility than simply tending to the horses. That's menial work. Your lover ought to have more standing. And it will relieve you of some of the heavy burden you carry.'

"The queen is flattered to be referred to as his lover. She hesitates for a moment but is swayed by her desire to please him. Had she been of sounder mind she would have detected Sedeth's intentions. But she is a woman with a mission—one of proving to herself, to Sedeth, and to me, Nur, that she is feminine.

"'If you want my white steed, you shall have it. I am a woman who keeps her word. Follow me to the stables.'"

Nur laughs. "I can visualize her, even now, her legs apart, her body taut and masculine, proving she can be trusted."

I enjoyed Nur's humanness and laughed with her. "Sedeth must have been proud of his manipulation."

"You're right. He was."

"'How easy this will be,' Sedeth thinks. 'I'll be out of here sooner than I expected.'

"The queen rides with him around the land known as the matriarchy. At each post she introduces him to the warrior women

guarding the land. They're perplexed at the queen's display of love for the young man, but they don't question her actions. They rationalize that it's springtime, and that their queen, too, needs an outlet for pent-up emotions. They smile indulgently as she leaves.

"*They return to the queen's quarters toward evening. In her hut, he reverses the procedure of the preceding night. He encourages her to drink excessively. In a short while, the queen is intoxicated. She crawls on top of Sedeth's body, yanking at his sexual organ to arouse his desire for her.*

"*While she's engaged in her idea of loveplay, he thanks her profusely for the gift of the horse and encourages her to lie next to him. She's ecstatic, feeling desired. He urges her to drink more as he commiserates with her about the problems of the community. She complains endlessly until the alcohol overtakes her.*

"'*Good!' thinks Sedeth. 'This is how I want you to remain for the rest of the night.'*

"*She sleeps, stupefied, as Sedeth goes to the stables to saddle the white steed. He makes friends with it until he feels comfortable getting on its back. He rides into the night until he comes to the first post. A few words of greeting are exchanged with the warrior women at the post. They recognize him from their previous meeting and allow him to pass on. They wonder why he's riding at night, but since they'd been informed by the queen that he would be checking their posts, they think little about it. He continues riding outward, from one post to the next, until he's passed by all of them.*

"*In the blackness of the night, he rides beyond the frontier of the matriarchy, to find himself in unfamiliar territory. Sedeth increases his speed and, looking up at the moon and stars, realizes that much time has passed. Eventually he sees a light in the distance. It shines from a small, isolated hut.*

"*He dismounts and knocks on the door. It's the home of a friendly old man who has not been visited for a long time. He welcomes Sedeth, gives him food and drink, and provides grain and water for the horse.*

"*In the morning, Sedeth awakens and looks out into the vast, beautiful fields surrounding the old man's home. He stretches his body and yells at the top of his voice: 'Nur, I'm free! I'm away from the queen! Why can't you be here with me?'*

"*The old man comes running, wondering what is wrong. Sedeth tells him with great joy that he had been imprisoned in the matriarchy for three years and is now free to return to his home. The* old man gives Sedeth directions, sending him on his way with an ample supply of necessary staples.

"Sedeth is ecstatic that he might soon see his kind, devoted mother. He prays that she is still alive.

"The trip to his village takes three days. When Sedeth enters the gates of the place where he had been born and lived for his first five years, he weeps. He looks for familiar faces among the inhabitants who are walking in the streets, but he recognizes none of them. They look at him with curiosity, but he is not familiar to them, either.

"He follows the path to his home. He stands at the entry, nervous but excited. He shouts his mother's name, the name he called her when he was a child. There is a silence. He shouts again. Soon, a gray-haired woman opens the door and stands at the threshold, peering at the intruder.

"'Kika? Kika?'

"They're no longer strangers. They fall into each other's arms."

"She strokes his face and kisses it while he clutches her, weeping. Sedeth cannot release himself from her embrace. Kika pulls him into the house. Once inside, she continues stroking his face and kissing him. All the while Sedeth is whispering, 'Kika. Kika. It's been so long. It's been so long.'

"She encourages him to go to his room, to wash himself and dress in clean clothes. She reminds him that by now he would have outgrown any clothes left from the past, when he would steal home from his foster family for a few days. She suggests that since he's a grown man, his father's clothes will be the right size for him. Sedeth hurries to his room and dons his father's shirt and pants. Bitter tears well up in his eyes at the fate that has befallen all of them. He hurries, despite his sadness, looking forward to the sumptuous meal Kika is making for him.

"Sedeth returns to Kika's kitchen, delighted. She sits with her beloved son, smiling radiantly as he eats. He tells his mother everything that has happened to him. Then, exhausted but happy, he falls asleep in his bed. His mother covers her precious son, telling him to be at peace, that not until tomorrow will they speak of graver things.

"Sedeth dreams of me. I intuit his thoughts from my disembodied essence while he's sleeping, letting him know I'm near. 'I've hurt you, Nur,' he says from his unconscious dream state. 'Help me get stronger.'

"I reply, 'To become stronger, you must face your weaknesses. We spoke about your deficient male energy when we were together.'

"'What must I do to change it?'

"'You'll find out as you live your life, as you make decisions, as you face yourself at every moment of existence,' I answer."

"In the morning, Kika tells Sedeth that his father's killer is still in search of him.

"'Your life, my dearest son, is still in danger. Know that your father's murderer is relentless—like one possessed. And now he has a powerful political position as well. It would mean so much to me if you could stay, but you know how dangerous that would be. Our lives have been difficult—yours, because you've had no home since the age of five; mine, because I've had to bribe my servants and those who housed you to keep you safe. My money is depleted. But we're both still alive, and for that I'm grateful. You'll agree with me that you must flee to save yourself.'

"'Oh, Kika,' Sedeth says in misery. 'I can't do it. I've run all of my life. I can't continue to do it.'

"'I'm old,' says Kika. 'I've not had much pleasure in living since your father's death. I'll not regret dying if your life can be spared.'

"He understands that he'll have to leave—this time for good. Sedeth, desperate for a normal life which would have given him the opportunity to develop a strong male energy, realizes that such a possibility is out of the question. How can he live a normal life when he's constantly in danger of being killed by a relentless enemy?

"They spend their last evening talking and giving one another courage to face the future. They hold one another, knowing it might be their last embrace. When the night is pitch black, a trusted servant and Sedeth set out in a wagon covered with straw, drawn by his mother's horse and the queen's white steed. When they arrive at the village gates, Sedeth crawls out of the wagon, mounts his white horse, bids the servant farewell, and embarks on the next stage of his life's journey."

"How active are you in his next adventure, Nur?" I asked, feeling weary from our deep concentration.

"Not very," she said, *"except toward the end of his life."*

"The end of his life? Is he discovered?"

"It's a long tale, Kendra. You don't seem ready for it."

"Perhaps I should wait until the morning. I'm fatigued and apprehensive about what's coming. In the morning I'll be fresher, more courageous. I'll reach out to you when I awaken."

"I understand," said Nur. *"It's exhausting to remain concentrated for a long time on such a high plane."*

"Thank you, lovely Nur. Thank you for understanding. I'm so happy to be in contact with you, my balanced self. But right now, I'm going to return to my physical body, which desperately needs to sleep."

"Good night, Kendra. Sleep in peace."

I feel the higher vibration around me disperse.

How interesting life is, I think, as I open the window to the warm night, fluff up my pillows, and give a last look at the flowers and plants that surround my bed.

I find myself floating away into nothingness. Nothingness is a state where there is no thought, just an indescribable peace. I breathe it into me. I revel in it, waiting for my entire being to be engulfed in it. I float happily, buoyant in this euphoria, until, with a jolt, I'm knocked out of it. The nothingness is now inundated by a tingly, bubbly, effervescent energy that begins to twitter around the room. I open my eyes and bolt upright.

"Ronald," I yell, my teeth bared from exasperation. "Leave me alone! Get out of my room! You may not be here physically, but I recognize your energy. Work things out for yourself. I'm not babysitting you! Find your male energy and live from it. I'm not helping you."

I push his energy away from my body, expelling it with my breath. I push it out the window with my arms and hands, out of my environment.

"God, Ronald! We're so connected, we're almost inside one another. Please let me sleep! Please! I'm going to hide underneath the covers so you can't reach me."

While I'm under the covers I sense through our telepathic communication that I can come out and he'll let me sleep.

"Thanks!"

I throw off the quilt, turn on my side, and sleep, at last, like a baby.

11
What a Death

The morning sky is overcast when I open my eyes. As I go about the business of dressing and having breakfast, I become aware of a high-level energy in the room. At first I feel it all around me. Then like a beautiful, composed bird, it wafts toward my left shoulder and settles there, sitting, waiting for me to take my last sip of tea.

I smile, delighted.

"Good morning, Nur."

"Good morning, Kendra. I know you slept well. I felt you exile Ronald for the evening. He's so anxious to be in your presence. Yet, as we both know, he continues to honor his six o'clock curfew."

"His behavior is what we in the twenty-first century call 'ambivalence,'" I explain.

"Whatever you call it today, thousands of years ago it was intrinsic to Sedeth's attitude toward women as well. That's why it's still present today, even though it's buried deep in his cells. You sense its presence. That's why you're behaving uncharacteristically, trying to keep your distance."

"Oh, Nur," I sigh. "You're so wise. It's difficult for me not to fall into his arms and take care of him. I've done this over and over with men in this life, and I've got to change a pattern that's given me few rewards and mostly pain. But I'm interested to go on with Sedeth's story."

Nur's energy leaves my left shoulder and pervades my entire being. I share my reaction with her. "It feels so good to be with you. I'm whole, larger, so secure."

"It's the real you, Kendra," she assures me. *"Feel her, know her. Reacquaint yourself with her."*

I become aware of being enfolded in a radiant, white light that expands my body to giant proportions. I'm an angel, balanced, connected to the most fulfilled energy that exists—

the energy of God. Tears flow from my eyes. I wipe them gently away and tell her that I'm ready to go on.

Nur is delighted. She continues with Sedeth's story.

"*Sedeth rides a long distance, to a village where people speak a different dialect, where they dress differently and comport themselves in ways that are unfamiliar to him. He arrives at an inn where he plans to spend the night. He orders food and drink from the female owner of the inn, a woman named Tiurne. She looks at Sedeth's handsome face and body and desires him.*

"*Exhausted and bewildered by his life's precarious twists and turns, Sedeth lets her take him under her wing. She offers him wages in return for taking care of the animals and serving the guests. He accepts. He's given a room next to hers. After the tasks for which he has been hired are explained, he retires to his room and falls into a deep sleep.*

"*Sedeth quickly becomes familiar with his daily chores. He serves the guests and jokes with them in a way that makes them all feel welcome. Tiurne looks at her handsome, blond, blue-eyed acquisition with pride. Sedeth is bringing business into the inn. The women who visit the inn, though few in number, return to stare at the young man who charms them until they're infatuated.*

"*Tiurne is covetous of her trophy, even though she has not yet been able to possess him sexually. Sedeth remains fatigued from his hard work during the day and falls into bed every night exhausted. He's never worked so hard, except for his time in the matriarchy. Before he goes to sleep, he thinks of me, though I've become a distant image, one he remembers with love but also with guilt.*

"*In this manner a year passes. Tiurne has become completely obsessed with Sedeth, but he remains unattainable. He is often curious about his lack of sexual desire, especially when he recalls our intense and frequent lovemaking. What's happened to himself? he wonders.*

"*One night when Tiurne suggests more emphatically than ever that they go to her room, Sedeth consents. She offers him the inn's strongest, most intoxicating drink. Sedeth, curious to find out about his sexual insufficiency, gulps down the drink. In a short time his usual barriers have been lowered.*

"*Tiurne undresses before him while he watches from her bed. He observes her efforts to entice him, but remains without desire. He can't rid himself of the memory of the queen's muscular, unfeminine* body. He's repulsed and pushes Tiurne away from him, with a lie to soften the rejection.

"'I can't forget Nur. I don't want to hurt you, but she's still with me. Give me time.'

"Tiurne lies beside him like a martyr. She feels flattered that Sedeth has accepted her at all. Sensitive to her needs, he puts his arm underneath her head, as he had often done with me. They sleep. He awakens during the night, slips out of her bed, and returns to his room. He wonders why his sexuality is so impaired.

"'Did you take it with you, Nur, to punish me for my weakness? Why can't I have a normal response to a woman? If, in time, I don't satisfy Tiurne, she's liable to throw me out. Then where will I go? I must make her feel more accepted even though she repulses me—the way the queen did. You never repulsed me, Nur. What's happening to me?' His thoughts remain questions without answers.

"Sedeth decides to spend every night in Tiurne's room without being asked. She coos like a dove. He forces himself to fondle her unappealing body, to which she responds with the lust of an animal. She fondles his genitals, but they remain flaccid. He thinks of me and of his unquenchable desire for me, but he can generate no desire for Tiurne, even though he superimposes my image on hers.

"Tiurne lies against him, panting with passion, wanting to be satisfied. Sedeth mounts her body, moving his limp genitals against hers. Overcome with excitement, she responds with ear-piercing howls and shrieks as her ecstasy peaks. Satisfied, she covers his body with kisses of gratitude.

"Sedeth is shocked at her reaction, shocked at his impotence, befuddled by his desperation and lack of male power. When Tiurne is ready to sleep, she presses herself to his body, unwilling to let him go to his room. Unhappily he complies, lying beside her, perplexed, miserable, and terrified.

"It becomes clear to all who come to the inn that Sedeth is Tiurne's property. Once again he feels trapped by someone else's power. On occasion, when he leaves the inn to make purchases outside their village, he feels her eyes follow him. He becomes overwhelmed by the trapped feelings her possessiveness invokes in him. His impulse is to run frantically into the distance. By running, he knows he would be able to dissipate his rage and terror. Instead, he controls himself and continues to do what he can to please her, paying little attention to his own needs and servicing her as though she were a queen. From time to time, she refers to him as her handsome, tantalizing eunuch.

"They live together for three years. Tiurne grows shrewish from sexual frustration. Sedeth, chained by his guilty memories of me, no more returns Tiurne's lust than he did the queen's. Yet he becomes increasingly subservient to the shrew, who has learned how to keep her slave under control. Most of the time Sedeth cowers in her presence, but he tries to please her so she won't be exasperated and throw him out. They're bizarre with one another in their private lives, but in the inn they are regarded as an ideal couple."

"Let's pause for a moment, Nur," I said, needing to breathe some fresh air. "It's increasingly clear from this story how little we move from old patterns to higher goals. Why does it take so long?"

"The time depends on the consciousness of the soul, Kendra. On how diligently a soul wishes to embrace a higher aspect of truth. You're familiar with this concept. How long did it take before you decided you had indulged enough in wasteful living and wanted change?"

"A long time," I answered, feeling ashamed. "It's actually only in this lifetime that I've achieved enough consciousness to make that choice. I don't mean to judge Sedeth and Ronald for their stuckness, but I'm impatient to move forward in a relationship. I'd like to experience being with a strong male while I relate as a beautiful, balanced female."

"I understand your need. But let's go on with Sedeth's story. Perhaps some of your questions will be answered."

"I'm ready."

"One afternoon Tiurne calls to Sedeth that he has a visitor.

"A visitor? Sedeth wonders. The realization that he's a fugitive, a thought never far from his mind, floods fearfully over him.

"He walks warily toward the entrance of the inn, where he spies a young man of about seventeen. Sedeth scrutinizes him from a distance but doesn't recognize him. He approaches the youth and asks, 'You wish to see Sedeth?'

"The young man is taken aback, but presents himself to Sedeth. 'I am Olin, sent by your mother. Here is her shawl, proving that she has sent me to find you.'

"Sedeth looks at the shawl and remembers that Kika had worn it on the day of his departure.

"'Is anything wrong?'

"'She's dying,' explains Olin. 'She begged me to fetch you.'

"Sedeth runs to give Tiurne the news. She helps him pack some clothes and food. They embrace and bid one another goodbye. She weeps quietly as she tells him, 'I'll miss you. The inn will miss you. Come back soon.'

"Sedeth looks at the woman who has given him a home in which he felt safe for the first time in his life. He is grateful to her in many ways and says so kindly, but he doubts if he'll ever want to return to the inn or to their life together.

"With Olin by his side, Sedeth begins his journey to his native village. During the three days of riding and nights of sleeping in fields or inns, Olin informs Sedeth of the many changes that have taken place. He speaks of the new village leader, whose name Sedeth recognizes as that of his enemy, his father's killer. Sedeth remembers Kika's mentioning to him that his father's killer had often come to their home on the pretext of inquiring about her health. He'd snoop around, looking for clues to Sedeth's whereabouts. He'd eye the servants suspiciously and when nothing was found, he would leave, frustrated, yet with a sinister smile on his face.

"Sedeth winces at the mention of his old enemy. His fear of being discovered flares up again. He questions Olin cautiously. The young man's response is brief and measured. It's clear from Olin's general conversation that the villagers admire the man, as does Olin. Sedeth is disquieted, but pushes the matter out of his mind and concentrates on seeing his mother before she dies.

"On the third day they increase their speed, finally arriving at the gates of the village. Olin leaves Sedeth, telling him that his part of the mission has been fulfilled. Sedeth feels a chill of terror run through his body, but shrugs it off, wanting only to see Kika. He rides to the house and dismounts. He knocks on the door, shouting, 'Kika, Kika, I'm here.'

"The door opens. Whoever has opened it stands behind the door, invisible. Sedeth runs to the center of the house, where he believes his mother will be. From the corners of the room appear men with black hoods over their heads, hatchets in their hands.

"Sedeth opens his mouth in what would have been a cry of terror, but no sound emerges. The men approach him with their weapons raised. In an instant the massacre is over. As the final blow is administered, Sedeth emits the bloodcurdling scream that has been stuck in his throat since he was five. The hooded figures withdraw. Their leader, an old man, appears. He takes off his hood and pays the murderers, who greedily take the money and leave the house."

"Oh, my God!" I cry. "Oh, my God! Sedeth, Ronald, what a death! I'm so sorry, so sorry! I feel so much pain! Nur, how do we go on living other lives or wanting to live at all after such a death?"

"We learn in painful ways. If we learn our lessons at all, we go on differently. If we don't, we repeat the same story with infinite variations, most of them worse. The universe insists on change and an expanded consciousness. The sooner the soul learns that this is the true rhythm of our lives and applies itself to it, the quicker we return to the Self."

12
Don't Be Hard on Me, Kendra

"Thank you, Nur, for your presence here with me. Thank you for revealing Sedeth's past. It helps to know about it. What I'll do with the information isn't clear. I'll need time to absorb it."

"I'll leave you now, Kendra," says Nur. "It's been a good visit. Call on me when you wish."

The atmosphere changed radically. It was as if I tumbled back into my body. I saw the flowers and plants around me. I touched my flesh. I'm real, I thought.

I came back to reality to hear a loud banging at my door, the door that was such a symbol.

Still immersed in Sedeth's story, I was shocked to hear a voice calling: "Kendra! Kendra! Open up! I know you're in there. I'll break down this glass door if you don't come and let me in!"

Ronald continued to bang on the door with such ferocity that I mumbled, "Aren't you overproving your male energy?" As I continued my descent to the basement, I saw Ronald's silhouette through the door.

By the time I arrived, he had a large crowbar in his hands, ready to strike. I rushed to the door, undid the latch, and opened the door slightly. He shouted in my face, "It's about time! Do you know how long I've been standing here yelling my brains out? Are you playing games with me? You accuse me of doing that with you?"

I was stunned by his forceful behavior. He reached through the crack in the door, got hold of my left arm, and somehow pulled me through the narrow space before I was able to withdraw my arm. Suddenly, I found myself outside, dressed only in pajamas and a robe. With gargantuan strength, he pulled me along the driveway, out onto the road.

He kept pulling me along rapidly, screaming, "I'm pissed off. Really pissed off!"

Good! I thought, not daring to vocalize my feelings because I was intimidated by his unusual behavior. Be pissed off, I thought. So am I.

"Do you know what happened to me in that life? Do you know what I went through?" he yelled as he continued to yank me along, looking at me belligerently. "If you say another word about my missing male energy, I'll . . . I'll destroy you!"

"You wouldn't dare!" I yelled back, pulling away from his iron grasp.

"You think I wouldn't?" he cried in rage, growing more energized by my response. "Do you want me to show you?"

"No! I don't want you to. Okay, what's bugging you? What happened? Why do you feel so sorry for yourself?"

"I had a terrible life!" Ronald said morosely, to my surprise, calming very quickly. "I've been on my own from the time I was five, had no love, had no real home, got caught in the matriarchy, went back to my mother's house, found an inn where I met Tiurne."

"You what?" I asked incredulously.

"I met Tiurne, who was another version of the queen. I was as impotent then as I am now. It was a horrible life." He stopped, looking at me directly. "Why are you staring at me with your mouth open?"

"I can't believe this," I gasped. "How do you know about the rest of your life as Sedeth?"

"It came to me during the night. I tried to reach you, but you pushed me away so hard, I had the feeling you were throwing me out of the window."

My mouth dropped open again. "Nur was also in touch with you? She and I were in deep communication last night as well as all morning long. That's why I didn't hear you knock. She was also with you! Oh, Ronald, we're so connected!"

I stood before him, amazed at life, amazed at the experience we were sharing, amazed at the man I was facing.

"Do you know how I died?" Ronald asked quietly, looking deeply into my eyes, trying to mesmerize me, bringing my focus back to him.

"How did you die?" I asked, even though I knew the answer. He was straining my patience.

"I was hatcheted to death like my father," proclaimed Ronald, with the air of a martyr. "Don't you think I have good reason to be terrified of living?"

Unable to restrain myself, I said, "Poor Ronald. Poor little, itsy-bitsy Ronald."

He shook himself out of his martyrdom and heard me. He became livid. I felt the rage catapult out of his pores. He wanted to demolish me.

I ran away as fast as I could. It was my good fortune that a pond was nearby. Difficult as it was to do, I shed my clothes while running. When I arrived at the edge of the pond, I dove naked into the depths of the water, holding my breath, hiding at its muddy bottom where he couldn't find me.

"Kendra. Kendra, where are you?" he shouted, stripping off his sandals and wading into the water, half irate, half frightened for my safety. "Kendra, stop playing games with me!"

I swam between his legs, throwing him off balance, so he toppled backward. He grabbed my arms and pulled me to him. "What do you mean, 'itsy-bitsy Ronald'? It was a hideous death!"

"I agree. But are you going to wallow like a victim forever?"

"I want some sympathy." His voice and expression were plaintive, as we stood in the water, face to face.

"You've been getting it from women for seven thousand years. Don't you think it's time for a different attitude?"

"Yeah, but have some sympathy for me, just a little."

I kissed him on his forehead, his eyes, his nose, his lips. He stood like a little boy, wanting more.

"Do you want to know what I really feel about where you are?" I asked, wishing to clarify things for both of us.

"Yeah," he responded petulantly, looking at me like a sheepdog.

"For God's sake, Ronald, enough. Strengthen your male energy and find some balance. You've been taken care of by every woman you've known. Your charm is too feminine, too soft. It has no backbone, no assertion. You're saturated in helplessness. I know, because I feel the temptation to take care of you. You'll never grow up if you don't recognize this in yourself and choose to move on. Nur was aware of this quality in you seven thousand years ago. Don't you think it's time to change your imbalance? I seem to be a catalyst for you. Use the insight and energy I give you to develop a higher consciousness."

"Nur was with me last night," he volunteered quietly and mysteriously. "She's such a wonderful being. I love her still."

"Aren't she and I one and the same?"

"Yeah, but she's not so hard on me."

"Because she doesn't have to live with your procrastination!" I yelled.

"Don't be hard on me, Kendra," pleaded Ronald. "I'm just waking up. You're a fraction ahead of me. I would be kinder to you if the shoe were on the other foot."

As if in spite of myself, I kissed him passionately. His eyes teared.

"I love you, Kendra, Nur," he whispered into my ear.

"I love you, too, Sedeth, Ronald."

"Let's get out of this pond," I suggested, "before we both turn into water nymphs." We clambered out and then lay on our backs nearby as the sun dried our bodies. We touched one another tenderly and kissed. We felt a beautiful closeness.

13
Why Can't It Be Right?

We lay side by side, holding hands, saying little. It was an interlude of peace, indescribably sweet. We were in ecstasy as the elements poured into our receptive bodies.

"It's so good," sighed Ronald.

"So good," I responded.

After a while, Ronald raised himself on one elbow and peered into my face. He asked aggressively, "What about you and your past?"

"Ronaaaald," I responded peevishly. "Are you starting up again? Can't we have a longer moment of quiet? It's either you're throwing a fit or you have to scurry off at six o'clock. Let's lie here and enjoy one another in a peaceful way. Just a little longer, huh?" The shoe was on the other foot. He had found a way to upset me. I felt peeved at having our tranquility disturbed.

He was quiet for a brief moment, enough for me to breathe easily and reenter a state of joy, then he erupted again with, "You're harping on me all the time about my lack of balance. What about your balance? Don't you want to share yours with me? You act so superior—as though you are the epitome of perfection. Well, you're not! Do you know how I know that?"

"No."

"Because if you're so together, why are you so devastatingly attracted to me? Either you've got a deficient male side like me, or you're on overload as a female."

I was on the verge of telling him "Out of the mouth of babes," but I bit my lip instead. I told him that I didn't feel superior, that I was not balanced, that I was more than ever aware of my unbalance. I told him that my intent now and all the time was to continue working on myself to achieve more balance.

But by now, I could no longer contain myself. I yelled back at him, "If I'm exasperated with you, it's because of your victimization and indulgence. I don't tell you that I haven't been in that state. I've been in it for centuries. I know what it feels like. But the further away I get from victimization, the less tolerant I become of its existence, not only in me but in others also. So if it will make you feel better, the intolerance I have is basically toward me. And the areas in me that are still unconscious. If I'm impatient, it's because I want this extraordinary connection between us to come to fruition.

"I've got a history of being too giving to the male—not because I'm a saintly person, but because I was afraid to face the tyrant in my female nature. The tyrant in me hated men. I would plot to destroy them for the slightest infraction and then leave them unexpectedly.

"To compensate for my murderous feelings, I overgave—to assuage my guilt. Do you think Nur didn't have repercussions from your betrayal?" I asked, sitting up to emphasize my words. "Do you think she gave and gave to you and remained unscarred by your betrayal? The soul doesn't function that way. It needs millions of lessons in rectification and redemption before it can 'turn the other cheek.'

"I'm in that process now, in how I deal with you. I love you, hate you, understand you, tolerate you, all these feelings—and, in the end, love you. I'm on a constant emotional roller coaster.

"At this point, I'm not terrified by the process because I've gone through it so often, always acquiring another piece of myself. Another piece of me gives me greater balance than before. This is the first life, I believe, in which I've arrived at a significantly greater consciousness."

Ronald listened attentively. I was impressed by his interest, which energized me to continue.

"And you know what? You're the recipient of all my efforts. That's why our connection is so important to me."

I was quiet, waiting for Ronald to respond. He said nothing for some time. I wondered how much of what I had revealed he had understood.

"I've heard what you've been saying, but what bothers me most is that you think Nur felt I betrayed her. How can she accuse me of betrayal in view of all the difficulties I faced?"

I lost my temper, then counted to twenty silently. By the time I answered I was red in the face, seeing, as if for the first time, how denial creates utter confusion and denseness in a person's psyche.

When I began my explanation I started it in first gear, then slowly accelerated to a barrage of truths about his life that must have been overwhelming.

"It was because of your narcissism, Ronald, that you misinterpreted the queen's attention and intention toward you. Because you cowered in the corner of your hut from terror as they mangled Nur's body. And because you slept with the queen after Nur's death.

"You also slept with Tiurne for the same reasons you slept with the queen—to feel safe, to feel secure. You gave your body to women whom you didn't love and weren't attracted to in order to have security. Your genitals are wiser than you because they wouldn't respond, and haven't since Nur. I'm sure they're not responding to your present queen, the woman you married fourteen years ago and to whom you run at six o'clock.

"You don't want to give to a woman. You want to be taken care of. You have a hole inside you where your heart should be."

"Leave me alone!" he screamed, bursting into deep sobbing. He ran into the pond, where he submerged his body, cooling off his rage and tears.

I lay on the side of the pond, feeling exhausted from my effort, realizing that once again the focus had returned to him. I prayed silently: Ronald, desire to wake up. Desire to have more of yourself than your victimization. Wake up. We have something precious. Don't wait to mend your inadequacies in another life. We'll lose one another again.

He came out of the water and lay beside me. There was a long silence. "I'm thick, Kendra?" he asked timidly.

"You're thick, but delicious," I told him, managing to ride more easily from the crest of the wave to the trough. I kissed him as a mother would kiss her child.

"Let's make a truce," I suggested. "Your resistance is exhausting. Let's call on Nur so you can become better acquainted with my female energy and hers as well. She'll give us information about my story. Do you want to call on her? That way we won't kill each other."

Ronald was quiet. He looked at me in such a loving manner, I began to cry. He held me close to him, rocking me, singing the last verse of our love song.

Ecstasy is ours,
two become one.
One never again two.
Living is complete.

We're so close, I thought while he was singing. God! My heart hurts so much! Why can't it be right between us? The answer that came to me was:

You are where you are.
You are moving
toward a different place.
Live through what
you are experiencing.
Achieve
another
balance.

Okay, I thought in answer to the wisdom I'd been given. I'll not stop; I'll keep fighting. What else could I do? I'd done it before and as a consequence attained more consciousness. So be it, my Lord.

I smiled at Ronald. "I love you, my erratic, growing, confused, strong, dependent, terrified Ronald. But now, let's call Nur, who will tell us about my past—my cuckoo, vicious, loving, wild, frenzied, powerful, erratic female."

"I want you, Kendra. Right now! I want you!" He devoured me as I accepted all his passion, erupting over me.

"Ronald," my voice trembled. "You're a powerful lover."

"That I am," he responded, his eyes twinkling, as he rested by my side.

Part Two

14
We Call on Nur

Once in my house, we called on Nur, who said, *"So soon, Kendra and Ronald?"*

"So soon, Nur," I responded. "Ronald wants to know about my female energy so he doesn't feel like he's the only one not in balance.

"I have to admit," I said slowly, "that I criticize him a great deal. Maybe if he saw some of my unbalanced female energies from the past, he would be encouraged to work more diligently on himself."

Ronald spoke up, asking Nur whether she had felt betrayed by his behavior seven thousand years ago.

Nur seemed perplexed by Ronald's question. Instead of answering him directly, she instructed us to close our eyes and concentrate. When we had done so, she asked if we were ready to go into the past. Our response was an emphatic yes and then she helped us open our third eyes. I was happy that Ronald went along easily with the entire procedure. We immediately felt an expansion in the center of our foreheads. Through that portal we entered another reality.

This reality was a misty one at first. Nur instructed us to enter it with curiosity and conviction. Slowly the mist lessened and figures in the haze gradually became clearer, until I recognized Nur's soul in the heavens. She stood by a large table around which were seated several figures who somehow exuded an aura of wisdom. They were counseling her about her next incarnation.

She was saying to the wise ones: "I do not wish to oppose your decision, my lords, but I am not anxious to be incarnated again. I am wary of another life, because the one I've come from was so difficult."

They observed this soul, knowing it was an elevated one but one that needed a stronger balance between its female and male energies. Her male energy had not been utilized in the matriarchy, creating the imbalance they were pointing out to her.

"If you insist I enter another life as a female, then I must tell you I am wary of men, particularly men who betray me. I am also wary of women who do the same. I go into my next life guarded, not open and loving as I lived my life in the matriarchy."

The sages listened and explained to her that she must find balance between the two energies, that her life's experiences would dictate how that balance would be achieved. She told them that her death had been terrifying, such as she did not wish to experience again. She explained about her betrayal by her beloved, who had not fought for her but succumbed instead to the enticement of an evil queen. She questioned how she could ever love again with so much woundedness inside her.

"At this moment, my lords, I cannot conceive of ever extricating myself from the rage and terror I feel toward human beings. I was so innocent, so filled with love for everyone. My innocence and purity of spirit were given to a humanity that had only the desire to eradicate it. You speak to me of achieving balance. In finding balance, will I lose my innocence? Will my innocence be tempered by Earth's reality?

"At this moment balance is unfathomable to me. I fear I will lose myself entirely. If you insist I go, then I go with trepidation. I go with anger and hatred. But I see also that I go with the intrinsic part of me—the purity of an angel."

The sages were impressed by her sincerity. They told her that all souls needed tempering. They told her that when a soul is called on to do the greater work, it must be balanced and tempered. It must have the wholeness required to be effective for the greater cause. The greater work and the greater cause needed an army of angelic souls who had experienced all matters. Their strength, their valor, and their integrity already must have been proven, giving them a place in the universe near the Essence.

Tears came to my eyes as I listened to the depth of Nur's simplicity and beauty. This is who I am, I thought. This is me. Nothing will stand in the way of my fulfilling my true nature.

Ronald too was deeply moved. "Wow," he said quietly. "You were hurt by me, Nur. I was blind to your pain and suffering, involved only in my own."

"You are both learning from my story," said Nur. *"Yes, Ronald, I was devastated and dazed by your cowardice, as well as befuddled by your inability to recognize the queen's deceit and treachery. I loved you nonetheless, but after my death, the terror of surrendering*

to a man became embedded in me. For centuries I related to men with rancor and vengeance.

"You see, Kendra," she continued, turning in my direction, "it was the beginning of my victimization. From that point on, every misdeed I perpetrated received commensurable punishment. Every punishment I received led to more mindless misdeeds and victimization. I now know that the initial wound is not healed by retaliation. I didn't know this truth then. I needed centuries to recognize it. At this moment, Kendra and Ronald, you are aware of how much you still struggle with that issue."

I nodded my head, as did Ronald, but because we were profoundly interested in her thoughts, neither of us wished to interrupt.

Nur continued. "My victimization began by my coming to Earth reluctantly. Coming to Earth reluctantly sets the ground for a defensive life. Feeling that I was everyone's prey promoted only one way of existence: to defend and to fight savagely.

"I became despotic in many lives. I used insanity as a way to ward off an enemy. I killed as well. I sometimes loved a man, but invariably I was again betrayed, because my discriminative abilities were warped.

"My soul clamored to be heard. I listened to it, but I defiantly cast its truth away. I survived in a willful defensiveness.

"I fear I might be boring you, speaking so much about myself."

We assured her that all of this was what we needed to know; that we were transfixed and moved, and wished her to continue.

"Since you want to know more about Kendra's female nature, which is of course mine, Ronald, as well as a part of who you are, I will demonstrate the effects my woundedness had on my behavior in other lives. Notice how one ungodly deed brings about another; how the perpetrator brings punishment upon herself through the retaliation of the victim, even though it might be in another lifetime. Notice how an endless circle of abuse, retaliation, and guilt becomes the being's way of life.

"Look at your lives, Kendra and Ronald. Look at the accumulation of evil. Observe how you were encased in defensiveness that kept you safe within your impenetrable walls—but so disconnected from your real selves."

Nur suddenly raised the energy level around us until we were both spinning. Ronald felt dizzy and nauseous. I waited for the spinning to cease, somehow knowing we would soon have a different, more elevated vision.

Nur instructed us to look ahead. We saw a waterfall cascading over large boulders. We beheld a shimmering rainbow reflected from the fast-falling water. The colors of the rainbow became more vibrant, moving around in the atmosphere until they crystallized, assuming various shapes and images.

I held my breath as I recognized parts of myself being projected from the shimmering rainbow. Ronald, who could not be contained, exclaimed, "Kendra, I see a part of you! You look different but you are still recognizable. You're getting clearer and clearer. You're beautiful, but wild and fierce.

"Is this real? It's like a movie. You're taunting a man who wants you. He wants to grab you. When he's close, you pull yourself out of his grasp and laugh. What a bitch! You mock him and then approach another man who's standing a short distance away. Kendra, you're a man-killer! You then take the second man by the hand and lead him into a room in a nearby house. All the while you keep your focus on the first man, a pathetic, taunted idiot who just sits and looks dejected. You know, that's a familiar feeling to me. You've made me feel that way a number of times."

"Nur," I called out. "Are his comments necessary?"

Nur didn't respond, which I took as license to try to bring more consciousness to Ronald. I said, "I perceive you now to be in a victim mode, Ronald, so you can't distinguish nuances in behavior. Do you know what that kind of obtuseness stems from?"

"No," he answered, challenging me.

"When you can't get your way with a woman, you feel rejected. But you never take into consideration what you did to warrant rejection! If you would get your ego out of the way, you'd be able to look at my female energy with some expansiveness. Otherwise this experience will be worthless. You must stop judging and look objectively at what your betrayal and cowardice did to Nur and to me. If you don't, we'll never achieve balance."

Despite my irritation, I looked at him tenderly, a look that pleaded with him to understand. He responded, "Okay, Kendra, I'll try. I guess I wanted to hit out at you, now that you're being exposed. I don't need to do that. Your lives will probably be devastating enough."

I winced, feeling an absence of the sympathy and rapport I wanted from him.

The young woman pulls the desired man into her room. She has passionate sex with him. He is overwhelmed and would have become her devoted slave, except that after he pays her, she pushes him out of the room, feeling victorious over her conquest. She counts the money she has earned and washes her genitals of his semen. She ignores her feelings of being soiled, contaminated, and ugly. Instead she revels in her power over the man. She continues living her life as a sought-after whore who makes a good living.

She becomes older and wearier. Her conquests of men grow less rewarding. She longs instead to be held genuinely by someone who loves her, someone who wants to see her true nature and who understands who she is. The man she has spurned so many times hovers around her house. Lonely though she is, she continues to reject him.

One day, after a lustful hour with a stranger, she discovers blood and pus oozing from her vagina. She immediately blames her last customer. That a man might have contaminated her brings forth her rage and venom, rekindling the early emotional wound around Sedeth's betrayal. She can't consciously remember the initial wound, but the hidden memory has lain inside her abdomen and heart like a grotesque monster, ready to strike. It has now struck, and it is she who becomes the victim of its horror.

She pays attention to the infection, washing it daily and observing its condition. She is hopelessly diseased, however. The disease spreads throughout her body, leaving her weak and helpless. She thinks vengefully to herself that she would gladly infect another customer, if only she had the strength.

Instead she lies in her bed, alone—gravely ill. The news spreads rapidly through the population that the town's favorite whore is dying. No one comes; no one asks about her. She draws the curtains over her windows, which under normal circumstances indicates to passersby that she is sleeping.

Her ardent admirer, always watchful of her, notices that the curtains have been closed for many days. Curious and concerned about her welfare, he goes to her door and knocks timidly. He hears a rasping command to enter. She has a high fever and is delirious.

He approaches her bed and sees she is dying. Her eyes ask for for-giveness as she points to a drawer in a bureau near her bed. With labored breath she tells him to take the money he finds in the drawer, spend some of it for her burial, and keep the rest for himself.

He brings it to her, but she insists it must be his. He looks at his idol of beauty and femininity with sorrow. She sees his love. With her last bit of strength she gestures toward the money and then to him. Her eyes close with gratitude that her life has not been entirely selfish.

He stands beside her and cries at his loss. He asks himself why he has felt so close to her. He realizes that she was the only woman who had tolerated his passivity and sexual impotence. She was the only woman who had been able to spark life in his penis. She has been cruel and contemptuous as well, but he would never forget her for her generosity in helping release his sexual energy. He would have given his life to remain close to her.

He looks at the money she has bestowed on him and thanks her silently for her generosity.

"That's one of your stories, Kendra," said Nur, *after the images disappeared.*

I was silent. I felt moved. I was overwhelmed that I, Kendra—Nur, a woman—had sought to gain power over men by becoming a whore. I closed my eyes, feeling deep shame. I wanted to hide myself from Ronald, from Nur, from the world. After a while I managed to say aloud, "What con-voluted thinking. Look how it backfired. Did I learn then that vengeance brings only retribution? How and what did I learn from that life?"

"That's a good question, Kendra. Let's go to the sages and find out."

Again I saw our soul, Nur's and mine, with this latest expe-rience as part of us, standing at the table around which the sages sat. They looked in my direction and asked what I, the soul, felt about my feelings of vengeance toward men. I told them those feelings had killed me. But while living that life, I had thought I was powerful, paying back Sedeth, all men, for their betrayal. Instead, I died alone, wanting desperately to be loved.

They listened attentively, nodded, and then ushered me to a place where I could rest and contemplate what I had experienced. It was a blissful place. I was dismally aware, however, that in a short while, I would have to embark on another life, hoping to have learned from the previous one, hoping I wouldn't make the same mistakes.

I was raw from the story. When I regained confidence, I turned to Ronald and asked him sweetly, "Do you think the faithful one was you, Ronald? Do you think I'm resentful of your limitations in this life because we've already been here in other lives?"

"Yeah," he pondered. "Probably. You're not overly patient. My wife is more patient than you. Maybe that's why I'm still married to her."

I held my breath in an effort not to cry. When ! felt in control of myself, I said calmly, "If you're going to be a mean, sarcastic cuckoo bird, we're wasting our time. I don't want to expose my female energy to someone who wants to use it against me. I want understanding from you, and com-passion."

"I'm giving you back what you gave me," he replied soberly. "That's how I perceive it. I guess my wife and I live a fairly monotonous life, compared to my relationship with you. She and I don't confront each other. It isn't that we don't have issues, but somehow they get dissipated and forgotten. With you, it's an explosion every other sentence."

He suddenly stopped talking, sensing I was pained by his defensiveness. He gently stroked my cheeks with his hands, looked deeply into my eyes, and confessed, "You know something, Kendra. Despite the constant upheaval between us, I'm not the same. I'm growing. You challenge me all the time."

I took his hands from my cheeks and kissed them gently, gratefully.

"But does growth always call for so much drama?"

"I don't know, Ronald," I said thoughtfully. "Look at my past life. It's the essence of drama: disease, death, hatred, will-fulness, revenge."

"Why does living have to be like this, Nur?"

"The soul is wise," answered Nur, "but the being, with its accumulation of misdeeds, requires time to work through its lessons. Consciousness is not achieved instantly. As a matter of fact, in the heavenly spheres it's known that a soul can have as many as a thousand lives before the slightest spark of consciousness is achieved."

Nur then turned to Ronald and told him: *"You and your wife might be too afraid to face your problems directly, and that's why you live superficially with one another."*

"Maybe," he responded sadly.

"Kendra," continued Nur, "after you looked at your last life, you thought you'd be free of further recriminations toward men. Let's look at another of your lives as a woman. Perhaps you'll begin to understand how dense, how defensive the unconscious is. I've always had the feeling that bringing the unconscious to consciousness is like trying to move a mountain."

"That's exactly how I feel right now. But I need to wait a bit before going on. I feel tired and sleepy. When I get like this, I know I'm resisting taking in more about myself, but taking it in is not easy. What a bitch I was—such a determined, but lost woman."

I playfully turned to Ronald and pinched him on the shoulder. "From time to time, I get inklings that I can be that way."

"Ahuuh!" chirped Ronald under his breath, barely audibly. "Ahuuh!"

I gently punched his shoulder this time, just vigorously enough to make him aware that his utterance had not passed me by. He caught my hand and kissed it lovingly.

I sighed gratefully. His thoughtfulness gave me the boost I needed. "You're not disdainful. I'm glad. Thanks." I was ready to move on.

"Are you coming with me, Mr. Ahuuh?" I asked, smiling at him.

"Ahuuh," he grinned. "I wouldn't miss it."

I ignored his undisguised sarcasm.

We turned our attention to the waterfall. This time the waterfall and the shimmering rainbow were moving with such force and velocity that they looked as though nature had gone berserk. We asked Nur if our perceptions were betraying us, or if the scene really was that different from what we had grown used to.

Nur told us we would find out, and to keep our eyes fixed on the movement of the water and the shimmering rainbow. Gradually they both became imagery. The imagery steadied itself. It was then that I began to understand why so much turbulence had occurred.

A middle-aged woman
at the time of the witch hunts.
She has been imprisoned for a long time.

The atmosphere in her village
is one of terror.
Whoever speaks the truth
is burned at the
stake.

I've been incarcerated for
speaking honestly.
I'm in a cold corner of an
antiquated jail cell—
a very large cell that's so
dark I cannot even see
the opposite wall.

I hear the rattle of keys
inserted into the door lock.
A soldier enters.
I look forlornly at him and
realize dimly that a new prisoner
is by his side.

"Who is it this time?" I wonder,
unable to see her clearly.
"Has this poor victim spoken her
mind, as I did six months ago?"

"You're only fourteen years old,"
the soldier says as he pushes
the captive forward.
"You should have known better
than to have a loud mouth."

She must have resisted him. I
hear his cries of annoyance.
"Move along, hurry, don't try
your tricks with me."

She remains silent.
They have apparently arrived at the
spot where she will be left.

Silence—creepy, awful silence.
I hear a bang, as though she were
thrown to the ground.
Then a shriek of agonized pain.
The soldier, of huge proportions,
must have thrown himself on top
of her.

Soon after, he grunts like a pig.
I see him pass me by, buttoning
his trousers.
With raucous bravado, he tells
his comrades outside the cell,
"Another tender fawn."

I place my hands over my eyes.
Reality disappears.
I throw straw over my body
so as not to see or be seen.

But the gnawing question arises:
"Should I go to the child who has
been ravaged or should I stay
safe underneath the straw?"

I convince myself to go to the
victim.
Unexpectedly the cell door is
opened again.
Two burly soldiers enter,
looking for the young girl.

They spot me, though I'm almost
invisible.
"Where's the virgin?" they ask.

I point to the place where she was taken.
The one who asks the question
looks me over.
He tells his comrade:
"She's too old.
Let's look for the younger one."

I sink back into my straw,
a mixture of terror and guilt.
I hear the screams of the girl.
They do not stop.
She's raped again and again.

When they're satiated,
the soldiers leave the cell.
My teeth chatter from terror.
I hide my body.
I groan from panic, wondering,
"What if I'd been the young girl?"

"Get up! Help her!" my soul
commands.
"You'd want help if she were you."

I crawl the long distance to her
side.
I see her disheveled body,
stained with her own blood.
When I look closely at her face,
my eyes bulge with horror:
It's my daughter, Maria!

"Wake up, Maria! Wake up, my
child!
I didn't know it was you!
I've been imprisoned for such a
long time that you've become
just a memory.

"Wake up, Maria.
I'll kill them for this.
I'll strangle them one by one!
Wake up! We'll escape together."

I shake her limp body.
Her face looks grotesque.
The soldiers had bitten her lips until
they were bloodied and disfigured.

"Enough!" I scream
as I raise her dead body from the
ground.
I fling it over my shoulders.
I stumble to the cell door,
my feet banging against the
lock.

The door magically opens.
The sun hits my eyes.
I can't see clearly.
No one interferes—
they're dumbstruck by the
sight that greets them.

I've become like a demented
animal, shrieking, howling as
beasts do in agony.
I walk steadily into the soldiers'
midst.
My ferocity stuns them.

They back off, awestruck, guilty,
fearing reprimand by their superiors
for their murderous deed.

I see a horse and wagon.
I place Maria's body
onto the wagon bed.
No one stops me.
I hold the reins and with one
last howl ride into the distance,
far away from those heinous
others—
creations of the devil.

We ride a long time,
until I see a cave.
I bring Maria's body into it.

That night I sleep by her side,
holding her stiff, cold hand.
I think: "By morning, you'll
waken, my little girl. This is
only a nightmare."

The light of a new day comes
into the cave.
I turn to my beloved child,
"What will you have to eat?
I'll fetch it for you, my darling."

I walk a few miles until I reach
a farmer's field.
I pick vegetables, devour
them whole, and take some
for my daughter.

I see cows.
Their udders are swollen.
I place my mouth to one of
them and drink the milk it
offers.

I stumble around, my eyes
wild and frenzied, looking for
a container to fill with
milk for my child.
A farmer, gun in hand, approaches.
He asks,
"What are you doing here?"

Stunned, bewildered, not to be deterred
from my mission of feeding my
Maria, I leap toward him like a
lioness.
He shoots at me but misses.
I run away. I hide behind
a tree.

"Crazy woman," he screams.
"I would have given you food
if you had asked! Come back. I
won't harm you."

I stay hidden.
Two soldiers appear on horseback.
They've heard the commotion.
They ask the farmer,
"Have you seen a middle-aged
woman, totally mad? She was seen
coming this way."

"I haven't," the farmer replies.
"Speak up. Don't lie to us."
They surround him menacingly.
"If you're protecting her, you'll
be taken by us. The fire will do
the rest."

I creep stealthily toward the soldiers.
I spring upon them and
knock them to the ground. We take
their rifles, bludgeoning them
until they are dead.
I'm dazed and exhausted. I help
the farmer bury their bodies.
I say,
"I must go back. I must feed my
child."

He takes me on horseback with
milk, meat, and vegetables to the
cave where Maria and I
spent the night.
I introduce him to my daughter.
He gasps when he witnesses my
attempt to feed the corpse.
He says,
"Dear woman, your daughter is dead."

I look at him in utter disbelief.
But I know somewhere in my
demented brain that he speaks the
truth.
I grab his rifle.
I kill myself before he can stop me.

I cannot—
will not—
look upon
my cowardice,
guilt,
and
shame.

The imagery stopped. I was silent and thoughtful. "Is this an aspect of you, Kendra?" asked Ronald. "What animal fury, what passion, what dementia! It's hard to detect at all in you nowadays. You must have worked very hard to bridle such violence."

"Yes," I admitted quietly, thinking of all the years, all the agony I had undergone to recognize that such a character was in me. After a long, painful silence I said, "It was a mammoth undertaking not to deny her existence. But if I hadn't acknowledged her in me, I would have remained untrue to myself. Once I accepted her energy as mine, I had to find ways to use it—to use its power, transform and balance it. That's what I'm working on, Ronald, all the time, every day—so I can be who I really am. Being who I really am is of the utmost importance to me."

I looked at him tentatively, assessing carefully whether I should make my next statement. I decided I would. "I hope that same kind of need becomes a part of you."

Though he ignored my subtle plea, Ronald was impressed. He asked Nur if all the fury I'd shown in my last witnessed life was a result of his betrayal.

"Most likely," Nur answered. "Fury begets fury. One misdeed begets another, until the wheel of destiny is so overloaded that consciousness remains buried in the debris of unconsciousness."

"How does one move out of such a state?" I asked.

"It happens almost serendipitously," counseled Nur. "It's not accidental, really, because years of search, exploration, and rebalancing coax a clearer consciousness out from its hiding place. It's like striking a match over and over until at last a light flares. The light becomes brighter and brighter until the person seeing the light no longer wishes to remain in darkness."

"Can I get to this place, too?" asked Ronald, feeling left out.

"It's within your grasp," said Nur.

Ronald looked at me, disturbed, wondering silently if he could catch up. Intuiting his fear, I squeezed his hand and told him, "You have to—you're a part of me. Do you always want to be dominated by the female?"

He shook his head. I was delighted. We both looked toward Nur.

"The soul becomes a seeker—a seeker for its intrinsic self. You'll be witness to this truth in your next life, Kendra."

In my next life? I thought to myself. I couldn't fathom taking in another life. I was in a state of shock from the last two lives. I kept repeating to myself: The soul becomes a seeker—a seeker for its intrinsic self, the soul becomes a seeker . . .

Ronald heard my mumbling. He shook me. I looked at him with dazed eyes and uttered almost inarticulately, "I need to process, to feel those two women. I need to feel them in me. I need to feel their ferocity."

"What's she talking about, Nur?" asked Ronald.

"Let her be, Ronald. She's in their natures, feeling and identifying with their natures so she can familiarize herself with their energies."

"What's the point of that?"

"When you recognize an undesirable energy, you can change it, transmuting it into good, wholesome energy. You can physically move as the unwanted energy urges you to, doing so in an expressive manner, feeling the full extent of its power, and then release it from your body. When that has been accomplished, the next step is to visualize how your psyche feels without that energy, when it's more balanced. Visualization that is accomplished when energy has been transmuted can bring about transformation."

"I think I understand," said Ronald, feeling inadequate.

"Don't worry, you'll catch up. The process that Nur's talking about might take a long time, though. Please put a blanket over me."

"You're throwing me out before six o'clock?"

"Ahuuh," I said in my half-dazed state, smiling lovingly at him.

"Okay, Kendra, but I'm going reluctantly."

"I know, Ronald. Let me do what I need to do."

"Let her be, Ronald," urged Nur. "We'll see you tomorrow."

"Thanks, Nur," I told her gratefully.

"Get to work, Kendra," Nur instructed. "All this information is a gift—a gift, putting you ever closer to your intrinsic self."

15
Time Off

Where am I? I wondered when I opened my eyes the next morning. I had fallen asleep with my clothes on. Ronald was bustling about in the kitchen, making tea.

"How did you get in?" I asked, astonished at his presence. "Were you here all night?"

"Not really. I left the door unlocked when I went home and let myself back in at the crack of dawn. I couldn't sleep because I was worried about you. I've been sitting here watching you be in what you call your processing state. You're really beautiful, Kendra. I fell in love with you all over again. You're so earnest and pure—just like Nur. You're getting more pure every time you discover another part of yourself. I hope you won't leave me behind and want nothing to do with me."

As he gave me my favorite tea in my special cup, his consideration and compliments touched me so deeply that they brought tears to my eyes. I felt I was still mumbling, though, as I spoke about the visions.

I confessed, "The ferocity of those women is still in me, Ronald. But now I feel I have a handle on that energy. Doing what I did—until I fell asleep—creates greater awareness in my psyche. I'm hoping that now all kinds of warning bells will ring when the ferocity takes over again. That's transformation—and it feels glorious."

Ronald sat transfixed. My process was his process. He insisted I eat the eggs he had made, hovering over me while I devoured the breakfast. I felt close to him and asked apprehensively, "Would you like to see a watered-down physical version of those women from the past?"

"Sure."

I hunched over, bared my teeth, rose from the sofa that I'd been sitting on all night, and screeched until my face reddened and the veins almost popped out of my temples and neck. Then I let loose with the worst profanity I could come up with.

Ronald backed off from me as though he'd been struck by lightning. He headed for the door. When I saw his reaction, I was shocked and embarrassed. Quickly I regained my former equilibrium and explained, "Can you imagine where I'd be if I were not processing such feelings, if I were stuck in them and they flared up unexpectedly? That's what my mother did. And when she held them back, she became riddled with cancer cells and finally died of that horrible disease."

"Kendra, you really scared me!"

"I know. I'm sorry, but that ferocity is what once helped me stay alive."

Ronald couldn't sympathize. He was unfamiliar with his own unacceptable, horrible feelings, so he judged mine.

I sat back down and continued to sip my tea while he looked at me, stunned. I felt like a leper. I realized I couldn't involve myself in another life. I felt nauseated, humiliated, exposed. I needed a break from our probing.

I took a shower, then returned to the room. I announced to Ronald that I required some time off, the rest of the day, in fact. "I'm not up to going on with more lives."

He was upset. He'd made arrangements with his wife to stay the entire day.

Too bad, I thought, but said nothing.

He argued with me. Afraid of letting the wrath of the last character take over my psyche, I took the car keys from the drawer and bolted out the door, driving away like a madwoman. I drove away from more insights, more scrutiny. I drove away from my continuing effort to understand and be loving to a man who couldn't be equally caring.

I drove mindlessly from one small country town to another until eventually, in one of them, I became aware of music. I followed the sound to the outskirts of the town. A carnival was in full swing. I parked my car, went to the box office, and bought several tickets to rides and sideshows.

This feels right, I thought. Now I can have some fun and be the child I never got to be.

Without a care, I used a ticket to enter the first ride I came to. It started and I found myself in a car among a sea of cars, each car bumping into the others, with nobody concerned about being hurt or hurting others. "Good," I thought. "This will release some of my pent-up emotions."

I enjoyed dodging various cars and then unexpectedly being jostled by other cars behind me or to one side of me. I laughed with glee. I headed toward a car in front of me, driven by a boy about seven years old, whose father sat next to him.

"Watch out, Joseph," his father warned as I drove toward them. Joseph skillfully got out of the way and hit the side of my car. I backed up and headed for his car. "No, you don't," screamed Joseph. "Yes, I will!" I yelled back.

We were in combat, all of us laughing with delight. With each bump received or given we let out a resounding "Huh! Huh!"—much like two warriors in the heat of battle. Then the cars stopped abruptly. The ride was over.

The three of us returned to the entry together and introduced ourselves. Joseph spontaneously took our hands and led us to the "spooky" tunnel. We all sat in one seat, Joseph in the middle. We were terrified by headless monsters that popped out at us from nowhere. The ride then catapulted us into an abyss filled with eerie, slimy creatures. Joseph held my hand, at the same time shouting with excitement, feeling safe and secure sitting between two people from whom he derived comfort and security. I relished everything that was happening and released the innocent little person inside of me to Joseph's experience of feeling safe and happy. When we all had met our last monster, Joseph stood up in his seat, shook his fist at the figure, and told him, "You can't scare me!"

"Nor me!" I added with zeal. We were beaming when our cars exited into the daylight.

"That was great!" Joseph exclaimed with delight. "What's next?"

"How about a whopper of a hot dog?" his father suggested.

"Yeeeah!" shouted Joseph. "You'll come along, Kendra?"

"Sure," I told him. "I haven't eaten one of those in years."

We sat together, our hot dogs covered with mustard, relish, and onions. Joseph kissed my cheek, his lips full of mustard. I did the same to him. He then gave me a relish kiss mixed with onions. I did the same. The father watched the two of us laugh uproariously, wondering which one of us was the bigger child.

When the time came for me to leave, they accompanied me to my car. Joseph hugged me with his child's strength. I returned the hug and told him, "You're the greatest, Joseph! Thanks for reviving little Kendra inside me."

"She's great fun!" he declared as they left.

She is, isn't she? I thought on my way home. Love brings her to life. Joseph was interested enough to connect to her. Few people even bother looking for her, however. I heard myself say, "I love you, little Kendra, foundation of my self."

I noticed that it had grown dark and six o'clock was long gone. When we arrived home, little Kendra and I crawled into bed, holding each other. It was wonderful. I felt that as a team we could tackle anything. I showed her parts of my madwoman. She laughed, aware that this part of me was my wounded, defensive self and that the real Kendra was evolving.

We slept soundly.

16
Kendra's Rebirth

I had breakfast alone—that is, with little Kendra. Afterward, I phoned Ronald. "Hi, let's go on with the stories." I ignored his peevish response and told him to come over quickly if he wanted to participate in the next one.

I went into the bedroom, sat against the headboard, and called to Nur. I palpated my third-eye center and the energy center on top of my head and waited for her to become available.

In an instant, the room changed and was filled with a most joyful, warm atmosphere. Nur was present.

"Good morning, Kendra. You had an amazing day yesterday—both of you."

"Yes," I responded. "It was a miracle, and just what I needed to do."

Ronald slipped into the room quietly and joined me, also sitting against the headboard.

"Are you both ready to participate in another story?"

"Before we do that, don't you think you owe me an apology, Kendra?" Ronald asked, turning to me.

"No. I did what I had to do and that's all there is to it."

"Okay, be weird."

"His comments don't affect me the way they used to," I told Nur. "I now have more of myself, and I can't be put into someone else's pressure cooker as I could before."

Ronald was ready to explode into a million pieces, but he contained his wrath and sat quietly next to me. I would have relished his explosion. In blowing up, he would have been more real.

"Your processing of the ferocious characters in you plus your connection to little Kendra have given you another quality. Do you feel the change in yourself?"

"I feel changed, Nur. But I'm anxious that I won't be able to sustain it."

"That's a legitimate fear," she explained. "But trust the power of your intentions—your intentions to purify."

"I feel a change in her for the worse," Ronald volunteered.

"Oh, dear," I moaned, realizing I would have to placate Ronald. "I'm going to look for little Ronald," I said, facing him playfully. I opened his mouth wide, treating it like a cave in which little Ronald was hiding. "Come out, come out, wherever you are," I said into the imaginary cave, my fingers pushed against his teeth and lips to keep his mouth partially open.

Ronald, without warning, jammed his mouth shut on my fingers. I let out a howl of pain, at the same time smacking him fully in his face with my other hand. He turned me on my back and kissed me hard. I softened and was jolted out of my anger at him.

"I missed you, Kendra," he told me. "And if I hurt your feelings, I'm sorry."

"You did—by judging my neurotic women. You punched me in the gut while I was down."

"Forgive me. They did overwhelm me. It's amazing how far away you are today from that ferocity."

"You see the change? Honestly?"

"I do."

"Do you really?"

"I really do," Ronald told me sweetly, sitting next to me, folding his arms around my body.

I put my head on his shoulder, feeling my hurts healing.

"Well!" exclaimed Nur. "Your emotions have made a full circle." She was giggling. "Now, are you ready to participate in another story?"

We both giggled with her and nodded our heads.

The energy in the room became vibrant. We saw the waterfall and the shimmering rainbow explode with images that bounced all over the cascading water. They were so numerous and so energetic that Ronald and I laughed like little children trying to catch soap bubbles in the air.

"Slow them down, Nur," we shouted, laughing joyously, waiting for recognizable forms to emerge.

After a while, Ronald yelled, "Not again! You're a whore again? It's another country and it's taking place in the time of Christ."

"How can you tell?" I asked.

"I don't know. The setting feels familiar. You're washing. This time you're washing yourself in a river. You're really cleaning up. Where are you going?"

"I don't know," I answered.

I'm sprucing up for a special occasion.
I'm still untamed and fierce.
I go to someone's house.
Others are entering.
A meeting is being held.
Most of the attendees are men.

I put my hair in order
before approaching the entrance.
A man asks,
"What do you want?"

I look at him belligerently.
"I want to go inside
and listen to Jesus speak."

"You what?" he sneers.
"There's no place for whores
at this meeting!"
He turns his back and
goes inside.

"Please!
I want to be near Him.
I heard Him speak before.
I want to come in and listen."

"You can't, because you're
not clean."

"I just cleaned myself at
the river. I want to come
in!" I shout.

He pushes me out of the
doorway and locks the door.
I bang against it,
to no avail.

I hear a gentle, quiet voice
wafting from the locked room.
I think in a frenzy,
"I must get near Him."

I climb a tree next to
the house. From the
branches I press my ears
and face against the walls
of the building,
and I can hear Him.
I feel ecstatic—
His words are entering
my soul.

I thrill to His voice, His
words. My body shivers
as I long to get closer
and closer to this man.

"Do I want Him sexually?"
I wonder. After all, I'm a whore.
"No! No! Not in that way.
It wouldn't satisfy my hunger
and yearning.

"What's happening to me?
Ordinarily I would seduce
a man until he'd scream to
have me,
and then I would make him
howl with
pleasure."

But there's something else here—
something my soul knows,
but my consciousness doesn't.

Right now I feel like a wild
animal,
impelled to dig a hole in
the walls of the building,
a hole large enough
for me to spring into the room,
to sit close to Him—
not touching Him—
just close enough to feel
His emanations.

"How unlike me this
is!" I think.
I place my body against the
wall, saying to myself
as if I am saying it to Him,
"You are my salvation.
I'll follow You to the end of
the earth.
You're mine, mine alone.
No one else can have You."

The meeting has ended.
People are walking out the door.
I climb down from the tree.
I run toward Jesus.
The men surrounding Him
push me away.
I stand, tears in my eyes,
watching Him disappear
into the night.

I shout repeatedly,
"I want You. I need You.
You're mine. No one else's."
I'm left with the echoes
of my longing.

My life is not the same.
I perform my whoring
duties perfunctorily.
The men sense it.
I don't care.

I follow Jesus wherever
He teaches. I watch Him
heal the sick. I stand
nearby—feeling too
worthless to be noticed.
But
I just want His love.

I'm voracious to receive
the energy He exudes.
His connection, I realize,
is to something
larger, something that
remains undefinable—
something my entire being
longs for.

"What is it?" I wonder
as I keep watching the man
who is more than a man.

I return to my life when
He leaves the area.
I've been uplifted, but
I am so lonely.
I become more reluctant
to sell my body.
I find the men gross,
insubstantial.
Life is unrewarding unless
I'm near Jesus.

I sit by myself for many hours,
remembering His words,
His simplicity, His honesty.
I begin to lose my old self
as I'm overtaken by His spirit.
I no longer recognize who
I am.

Customers are leaving me,
as are friends.
They want to hurt me,

but I walk away, remain alone,
thinking only of my love.

One morning when I awaken,
I feel a restlessness in the city
of Jerusalem.
I go to a neighbor's house for
the news of the day.
Three crucifixions are scheduled—
one of the men who will be executed
is called Jesus.

My heart stops.
"No!" I wail.
"Not Him! It must be another Jesus."

I rush to Golgotha.
I approach the hill with fear.
Three bodies are on the crosses.
One of them is that of
Jesus,
my Jesus,
who is already dead.

I rush to Him and scream out,
"Why do You leave me when I've
just found You?
Come down!
I'll love You forever!"

His family takes His body down
from the cross.
I approach them.
They push me away. They carry
Him off.
I ask silently,
"Why do You let them leave me out
all the time?
Why?
Why?
I need You so much!"

Tears stream from my eyes
as I watch those who seem

*worthier than I
to be close to His dead body.
I wonder if I'll ever be worthy.*

*Then I hear a voice piercing
my brain.
"You are not yet ready for me.
Keep looking for me and you will
find me. I cannot be yours
exclusively.
You must search for who I truly am.
Never give up.
Continue to search for me."*

*"I'm not ready!" I scream, as though
I've gone insane.
"I'm never good enough!
Well, if I'm not good enough,
I'd rather live in hell!"*

*My vengeance has no boundaries.
My mind has gone berserk.
I go to the home of the man who
prevented me from entering
the meeting.
I spit in his face.*

*Nothing can requite my sense of
betrayal, unworthiness, and exclusion.
I whore with greater zeal.
I take on more customers.
Each day becomes a challenge to
eradicate my newly found
Christlike self.
I spew forth hatred toward the
followers of Jesus. I report those
I've seen at His meetings.
They're promptly imprisoned.
My vengeance cannot be satisfied.
My pain cannot be avenged.*

*Slowly I begin to understand
that Jesus is not only a mortal man,*

but also a mortal man more elevated
than other men.
I realize painstakingly that He
symbolizes
the intrinsic self in each of us.

I think, "You took my new self with You
when You died.
This self was a fledgling—like a
baby bird.
I can't sustain this self without
Your presence. Your followers were
around You longer.
They absorbed Your teachings.
I'm just a beginner!"

I weep deeply, falling asleep
with images of Jesus in my heart
and soul.

I dream a memorable dream:
Jesus comes off the cross and
walks into my body. His Spirit
seeps into mine. I feel a self
that is greater than my ordinary
self. I become larger, a largeness
endowed with wisdom, beauty,
and courage.

In the morning I feel my new
dimension.
Jesus says to me,
"This is who you really are.
Live from this self. We are one."

I awaken transformed.

I no longer prostitute myself.
I seek out the homes of other
Christians and live with them.
We travel, spreading the good
news.

When eventually we are
imprisoned, I still hang on to
their memories of every word
and act of Jesus.

Ronald looked at me with awe. "God, we're so complex. We're like jewels inside—precious gems. If we've truly lived a thousand lives, as Nur said, how can we ever balance ourselves fast enough to recognize the pearls inside us and have them available? Does all of our evil have to be transformed, or can we sometimes take a shortcut?"

Nur and I laughed at Ronald's imagery. "If there are shortcuts, Ronald," I responded, "my life doesn't know about them."

"I'm just afraid I'll never be able to catch up to myself."

"Feeling as you do now, Ronald, is good," said Nur. "You have an urgency in you as never before to move more quickly, not to waste time. This is different from how you were a short time ago."

"Thanks, Nur. I feel more hopeful."

I added, "I've had to live through every grinding detail to get closer to my self. You're awakening. You're part of me. As a unit, you and I are lopsided because I've strained my female energy to compensate for your weak male energy. I want you to catch up so I can relax and assume my rightful place as a female in this androgynous makeup of ours."

"There you go again, Kendra," said Ronald, peeved.

"But that's the reality of our state, Ronald. If we don't face our lopsidedness, we'll remain that way forever. I want to achieve wholeness so we don't have to return to this planet. On a more evolved planet we might be able to exist without the constraints of this one."

"Is she crazy, Nur?" asked Ronald. "Another *planet*! What's wrong with this one? There's only one planet and that's Earth. We're living on it now, and we're going to come back to it. Stop making me crazy."

Nur entered the argument as a peacemaker. *"It's not unfathomable that there are other, more evolved planets on which life flourishes. But since we have no evidence of that as yet, we can use the possibility as a metaphor. Use it, both of you, to speed up your evolution. Know that you can be more balanced. Know that when you're more balanced you'll be called upon to do more evolved work elsewhere. Use it as a metaphor to help you be less indulgent, to push ahead, to leave no stone unturned as you seek your real self."*

Ronald felt put down. "I'm just a laggard," he said mournfully.

I tickled him, which made him laugh. We were both out of breath when Nur, also laughing, suggested we finish my story from the time of Jesus. She said our bantering had served as a good intermission because what was coming next demanded openness of spirit to provide healing.

"I'm scared, Nur," I said, upon hearing her cautionary note.

"No need to be, Kendra. You've already experienced all that happened two thousand years ago. Look at it, be refreshed, learn whatever lessons are contained in the experience, and move on—perhaps even to a better planet."

We laughed as we peered into the waterfall and rainbow ahead of us.

I'm in Rome—
twenty years later.
I'm an experienced missionary
to those hungering for the peace
and love of Jesus.

I see the Christians crowded
together in a cellar beneath the
arena. We're only women here.
The men were taken out of
the prison several days before
and never returned.

We all know it's time for
our combat with the hungry
beasts. I'm strangely quiet.
I feel fear occasionally,
but I'm too occupied with helping
others to allow the fear to
paralyze me.

Some of the terrified women
are helped by me and by other
women. We pray Jesus' prayers.
They feel relieved and become
more courageous.

I wonder where my strength is
coming from. The answer from
my spirit is that it comes from
within me.

I continue to have dialogues with
my inner voice.
"Oh, Jesus," I cry as the time comes
near. "Help me remain courageous.
Help me face this ordeal. Help me
remember that my conviction of
Your truth is indelibly imprinted in
my soul and that I'll never betray
Your truth,
Amen."

I see myself among many other
women being taken into the arena.
As we enter this vast space, I notice
crowds of people sitting above and
around it. We're jeered at by the
multitude. Their uproar numbs us.

I wonder,
"What are they jeering at?
My death?
Our deaths?"
The Roman women are convulsed
with laughter as they behold our
simple tunics, our uncombed hair.
I've taken my position before a post
to which a surly guard ties me with
ropes that cut into my flesh. I then
look at the faces of the murderers.

I see humanity in its most
horrendous state.

*"Jesus, what makes mankind like
this?" I ask, forgetting that not so
long ago, I was of their kind, with
their unconsciousness—
their hatred.*

*The crowd becomes silent.
A blast of trumpets precedes
the lifting of the gates to the
lions' cages. The animals run
into the arena but stop as their
ears are assaulted by a
tumultuous outburst from the
crowd. They become confused
by the human shrieks and howls,
and run back to their cages.*

*The guards prod them forward
until the scent of human flesh
takes them fully into the arena
and to their victims.*

*The first beast tears at a woman
whose shrieks of agony make
the crowd wild. They stand and
cheer, urging the animals to attack
even more ferociously.*

*It's my turn to be mangled.
I pray to Jesus that I remain
courageous and true to His words.
I pray,
"Jesus, my life, my truth,
my salvation.
Jesus, my life, my truth,
my salvation."*

*I feel a high vibration throughout
my being. I no longer feel my
body, even though I know a
hungry lion is biting into my
flesh. I'm out of my body.
I'm still aware, however,
of the voracious crowd.*

The men roar with glee as their
vengeance is inflicted on women.
The crowd continues to roar
until the whole spectacle comes
to an end.

I take my disbelief of humanity's
cruelty with me into the spirit
world. I transmute it as much as
I can. But I know that those
spectators in the arena will never
leave my consciousness.

I'm dead, yet at the same time
alive
and reborn to a newer, better,
more elevated self.
I'm not yet whole; my hatred of
humanity has not been
transformed.
I know there will be other lives in
which this necessary transformation
will have to be addressed.

I sat back against the headboard, eyes closed, tears rolling down my cheeks. My chest was heaving from the unbearable pain of having endured a crucifixion for my beliefs. I wanted to sit like that for a long time, experiencing my strength, my courage, my conviction. I wanted to feel the truth of my womanhood, my connection to my higher self. "Jesus, higher self," I prayed. "Help me remember my connection to You. Never let me lose myself again in the ways of the past. If I do get lost, hit me with a stick, like one would hit a stubborn animal, to pull me back from unconsciousness to consciousness. You are my consciousness."

"Kendra, Kendra," whispered Ronald. "Are you here? You're so quiet, so tender, so sweet. What do you feel? Talk to me."

I took a deep breath to imprint my prayer into my soul. I then answered him. "I feel purged, Ronald. Different. Closer to myself. It's an extraordinary experience."

I turned to Nur. "Will this state last? Please say it will. Do I have to die and die again in order to arrive at such a state?"

"You might," answered Nur. *"But once you taste that wholeness, that taste of who you really are, you'll strive for it, overcoming any obstacles and even dying for it, if need be. My dearest Kendra, that life was a rebirth."*

"I know."

I kissed Ronald, who responded with his heart. We were quiet. He took my hand and held it tenderly. He didn't want to release it. I felt he wanted to imbibe my experience and make it his. I knew he would have to go through his own experiences, though, and would be unable to graft my rebirth onto himself.

He heard my last thoughts in his soul. He released my hand, stood up, and told me he had to leave. His wife had asked him to do an urgent errand for her.

My heart pounded fiercely. I was divided between the lingering peace of my experience and my disappointment at his leaving. I made a conscious decision. I chose to follow my destiny, whatever it was, at the same time releasing myself from his.

How often have I done this? I asked myself, walking him to the door. I knew, however, that if I did not remain firm in my decision to go my own way, I'd soon be even more weary than before of his lack of resolve and his not moving forward.

He stood at the door, looking at me sadly. He wanted an eruption from me that would justify his leaving. After all, the only justification he might develop on his own would be that it would be wrong to hurt his wife. I knew he was going to live an unbalanced existence. He knew he would long for me, his other half, once he had retasted the other.

"Good night, Kendra," he whispered as he left, looking at me intently, hoping to be rescued.

"Good night, Ronald," I replied, at peace with myself, but aware that no one could save him but himself.

Part Three

17
Reorganizing the Energies

We stayed apart for a week. I convinced myself it was best that way, because it gave us time to reflect more deeply on ourselves individually and on each other.

One morning I decided to search for a clearer under-standing of how my female and male energies were existing in my body. I had always known that my female energy was overloaded, because my male energy, mirrored by Ronald's male energy, was weak and ineffectual. Soon I was tired of *thinking* about it. Instead, I moved my body according to the way these energies felt. I was also hoping to stimulate some powerful inner images.

I experimented before a mirror, starting with my right side. I had learned from my esoteric studies that the right side housed the male energy, the left side the female energy.

I lifted my right arm into the air, stretching it, and allowed my entire body to be moved by whatever actions that arm wanted to perform. It took on a life of its own, tumbling from one movement to another. But I became overwrought, impatient at the vague imagery I experienced while I was doing all of this.

I recognized my father's energy, though he had long been dead. I screamed in exasperation: "Get out of me, you weak, distorted, victimized coward! Get out! I hate your energy in me! I gave of myself to you at all ages. You took my love and adoration, bathed in it, and then discarded me like an old rag when you'd had enough. You took my precious love and went to her, your queen-bee wife, my mother, never looking back to give your daughter the merest crumb of appreciation.

"I continued to give to you, hoping you would accept me, but you were too scared to embrace me. What would she have done? Been jealous, been fierce with you? I gave and gave to an empty heart, while I stood like a beggar before you, examining the crumb you left in the palm of my hand. A crumb! A child on the diet of a crumb! I hate you and all the men in my life who have been like you.

"I didn't even know other kinds of men existed until the pain of your denial and rejection finally woke me up. I've always been magnetically pulled to your kind of man, father, and have spent a good part of my life repeating the drama you and I shared. Why? Because your energy was familiar; it was the only energy I knew. But a more profound reason for this magnetic attraction to your kind of man is that your weak, cowardly, unassertive male energy is in *me*! Isn't that a weird twist? It's in me!"

I'd done it again! Insight crowded on insight and I put them into words: Ronald goes home to the queen-bee and I, little Kendra, look on, alone, lonely, nurtured only by a crumb in the palm of my hand. I want you out of me, out of my life. I want a new, strong, powerful male—one that will enable my female to take her place in life and living in a balanced way.

I was furious and determined to change this energy. I strengthened it by moving like a charging bull around the room.

I screamed, "I don't want to be a coward any longer. I want strength. I can be assertive!" I charged from one end of the room to the other until my right side was energized, connected to its intrinsic power.

"Ronald, you came into my life as an outer-world representation of my male energy. In addition, we're attuned to one another because we've been together in other lives. Our attraction feels like it's love, but the bottom line is that you're not ready for love. This time I'll not compromise and take care of you. I won't pull you together while your unresolved nature exploits my caring, loving support.

"I'm making a decision: I want no more, no more of this inequality. For me, rejecting you is the equivalent of rejecting an ancient pattern that rules my life. Rejecting you will lead me to a stronger male—not only within me, but also to a male in the world who has such strength.

"I don't have to be stuck with you—even though I love you. I can love you as a friend. But as a lover you have little to give, and I'm starved for affection."

I moved my right side, stretching it from the hand and arm with such force that I felt I'd been released from centuries of imprisonment. "I'm free!" I shouted. "Yes, I'm free!"

After a moment, I continued, "Female energy, here I am. Are you ready for me? Where are you, overzealous energy, which took on the load of the male? I suspect you're afraid of strong male energy, fearful you'll be taken over, fearful of being receptive, fearful of being without your defensive weapon: the emasculation of the man. That pattern has been your way of living, your way of achieving power. I know you don't want to continue like that. I know you want to be your real self. Let me see you, female nature. Let me see your tenderness, your beauty, your inner strength, your embracing, surrendering wholeness. Let me see you and get to know you, my female."

I moved my left side, starting with my left arm, which reached toward the heavens. My body fell into a soft, round, open movement. It was gentle, clear, loving.

"There you are, my love," I said out loud, encouraging more tenderness to emerge as my body flowed smoothly from one movement to another. "That's you, Kendra. That's you, buried for centuries underneath all that defensive muck. Now move with grace and love. That's it! How beautiful! Why would you ever want to distort such qualities again?"

I walked around the room, first in my newly acquired male energy, then in my female energy. The two energies had a dialogue with one another:

> *She*: I want you to be strong so I can
> be soft and surrendering.
>
> *He*: I want that too—to be strong, clear,
> a wholesome male.
>
> *She*: I might fall back into my tyranny.
>
> *He*: I'll not back off. I'll help bring you
> back to your self instead. Will you do the
> same for me?
>
> *She*: With all my heart.

When both energies were clearly established, I lifted my arms above my head and joined my hands. I felt connected to my self and to life as never before. I was whole and joined as well to the Godself.

I sat on my sofa, invigorated. I realized that I'd had a week to myself, concentrating on me. The results were more than rewarding.

18
Ronald's Past Lives

My week of concentration on myself and the silence between Ronald and me had been fruitful. I was tempted to call him, but resisted it. Instead, I became aware of a powerful, uplifting energy around me. Nur is not present, I thought. What is it then? I palpated my third-eye center, the slow-moving door opened, and I saw Ronald in a small room of his home. He was pleading with Nur.

"Please help me. I'm afraid I'm losing Kendra. I must know how I've come to live with so crippled a male nature. Let me see my past lives. I can face whatever comes up. Please!"

"Very well," Nur answered, serene as always. *"Be aware that since you and Kendra are linked in an ancient soul history, she may experience what you see as well."*

"That's good," Ronald assured Nur. "I want Kendra to know everything about me. She needs to have as much information as I do."

"Look into the waterfall and the rainbow," came Nur's soothing voice. *"Relax and let the imagery pervade you, Ronald."*

"I don't see anything, Nur," Ronald told her, squinting his eyes.

"You don't want to see anything," was my immediate, distant response. I caught myself nagging him and stopped.

"You're trying too hard," suggested Nur. *"Follow the bubbles of the waterfall until they assume shapes. You don't need to prove yourself at this moment. Just enjoy what emerges."*

"I'm trying," Ronald answered, attempting to let go of his anxiety.

"Go for it, Ronald," I prompted from where I was tuning in. While I was giving him encouragement, I became aware of a vision of a tall, thin, foppish-looking male with a lace hand-kerchief in his hand. He was wearing a black velvet outfit and was very effeminate. I could almost smell the perfume on his body. His manner was cruel and vicious, and he used a wicked, sharp tongue against all mankind.

How did he get that way? I wondered.

Nur must have heard my thoughts, but remained focused on Ronald.

"What do you see?"

He was more at ease as he said,

> I'm three—
> in a modest house.
> I'm told not to go
> near my parents'
> bedroom.
>
> I don't want to be
> by myself.
> So I hide in their
> closet and peek
> through the keyhole.
>
> My mother's screaming,
> lying in a sweat in her
> bed.
> An older woman is
> putting hot compresses
> on her belly,
> which looks like a heaving
> mountain.
>
> "Why is she in so much
> pain?" I wonder.
>
> At a certain point my
> mother screams so loud,
> I'm sure she's being
> tortured.
>
> The old woman pulls her
> legs far apart and shouts,
> "Push! Push!"
> My mother's exhausted,
> but she pushes with every

bit of strength she has.
I know because I hear her
groaning and moaning.

All at once I see my mother's
vagina open up like the jaws
of a gigantic animal.
Out of it comes a head,
followed by a slimy, slippery
body and legs.

The old woman brings the
thing to my mother, who puts
it to her breasts. It sucks and
sucks.
"I wish I were doing that," I
think, jealous that I can't be
at her breasts, too.
"She never did that for me."

My father and several other people
rush into the room, stand by
the bed, and gape at the two
of them.
I rush to the bed, too, but they
take me bodily and plunk me
in a chair in the next room.
I'm alone—always alone.

From that moment on, I'm
considered a nuisance. I'm
left out. My newborn brother gets
all the attention.
They say he's handsome.
I guess they mean I'm not.
They say he's intelligent.
That means they think
I'm not.

For years
I'm ignored and shoved
aside. Even the servants
have no use for me.

"What have I done?"
I ask one of them, when
being alive no longer
makes sense.
"You're a bastard,"
I'm told.

"What's a bastard?"
The servant roars
with laughter and kicks
me in the buttocks.
"My brother's a bastard, too,"
I declare, innocent of
what I'm saying.
The servant, shocked,
tells my parents,
who now have reason
to send me away.

At the age of twelve, I leave
their household for good.
I ask my father,
"Why am I a bastard?"
He tells me,
"You were your mother's
mistake while I was
fighting a war. The sight
of you reminds her of her
wrongdoing. For this reason
you must leave our home.
You'll be apprenticed to a
rich artisan. He'll teach you
his trade and board you."

My father, for the first time
that I can remember, looks at
me with compassion, assuring
me,
"You'll be happier with the
stranger."
"Please let me stay with you,"
I beg. He turns his back and
reenters the house.

We're on the way to the
artisan's home.

I cry bitter tears, sitting
in the wagon
next to the servant.
"I don't understand why being
a bastard makes everyone
shun me."

"In the eyes of the world
you're damaged goods,"
he says, looking at me
sadly.

There was a deep, heartfelt silence for a long while. I sensed Ronald crying softly, saying, "Damaged goods in the eyes of the world. How horrible! And I was so young."

Nur asked, "Do you want to go on, Ronald? You're so pained!"

"I wish Kendra was here."

"Tune in and find her," Nur told him. "Open your third eye."
He did.

"Why aren't we together while I'm going through this life?"

"Because we needed a break, Ronald," I told him. "But I'm sharing this with you from home. You're experiencing a difficult life. Go on, though. I know you have the courage to finish it."

"Okay," he said, as though he had been revitalized. "I'd like to go on, Nur. But be available to me, Kendra. It's easier when I know you're around." He continued:

I enter a new home
and a different life.
The artisan is an old man
who lives alone—
he's been solitary for a
long time.
He loves his work,
that of making beautiful
furniture.

He, too, was apprenticed
at my age.
He looks at me approvingly
and gives me a clean room
in which to sleep.

He's a nurturing teacher and
I learn quickly. I become his
most valued pupil. In time he
imparts his treasured secrets
to me—those secrets which
have made him famous.

One evening, he comes into my
room and tells me about his
life. We become very close.
I need the love of a man.
I become confused, however, when
he begins fondling my genitals,
caressing them as though they're
his.
I tell no one about our intimacy
and wonder if every man and
boy enjoy such a relationship.

My body aches from my need
for sexuality.
I look toward young girls. They're
responsive to me. I'm invited into
a girl's room. She fondles me as
the old man has, except that I don't
get aroused. She stimulates me in
many ways, but nothing succeeds.
I leave her room,
feeling like a failure.

I confide in the old man of my
experience.
He laughs and tells me it had been
the same for him at my age.
He says,
"Eventually I gave up and put my
energy into my work. But you have me.

Come here. Let me fondle you
to see if you have that difficulty with
me."
I let him.

I find another woman who tries to
teach me. When it's time for me to enter
her, I become overwhelmed with
the size of her vagina, terrified I'll
get lost in this mammoth cave,
swallowed up forever.
I leave her bedroom,
again humiliated and ashamed.
I tell the old man.
Again he laughs knowingly.

He and I are intimate.
I have no difficulty
consummating my desire.
"I'm strange," I say to myself
afterward.
"He's strange, too. I've always
been so; so has he. It'll be our
secret.
"On the outside, I'll pretend to be
a normal man. I'll strut and be
menacing so others are afraid of
me. I'll look like a man."

The years pass.
As an artisan, I become more
proficient than the old man.
I'm sought after by
rich families to make their
furniture.
The old man encourages me
not to sell my work unless
the clients pay an exorbitant
price for my merchandise.
I become rich and famous.

When the old man dies, I inherit his
business and his money. I move to
an elegant house with servants. I
sleep in a four-poster bed draped
with silk curtains. I sleep on silk
sheets. I don velvet clothes, bathe
my body in exotic perfumes. I
become a caricature of a man, a fop,
a dandy
who thinks he's behaving
like a man.

I flaunt my wealth, adopt a superior
attitude toward those who are not
rich. I'm cruel to my employees. I
shun the company of women.
At night I sleep a deadly sleep,
dreaming horrible dreams about the
female body. I awaken in a sweat,
my legs apart as though giving birth
to a grotesque female animal that
resembles me. I scream out loud to
stop the dream, but it returns night
after night. I long for daylight to
come to escape from my hellish
nightmares and to resume living
from my comfortable persona of a
foppish male with a vicious tongue.

No one befriends me.
I like it this way.
My vicious tongue is like the blade
of a guillotine. I'm not aware of
how ugly my nature has become.

One day a high official from the
government comes to my premises
to purchase some of my valued furniture.
I give him my price. He looks at me
with disdain.
I flick my perfumed handkerchief
in front of his face and order him to
leave. He does.

A week later, soldiers arrive in front
of my workplace. They enter, come
face to face with me, tie my arms
behind my back, and take me to
prison.

I never become aware of the reality
of my situation. I never recognize how
offensive and cruel my demeanor is.
I'm so immersed in my
unconscious defensive state that I
do not even connect realistically
to my incarceration.

I die there, bitter, still a twisted
caricature
of a male and a human being.

Ronald felt a deep shame and was painfully reluctant to speak about that life. After a while he admitted that he was also living his present life split off from his sexuality, from his real need to love and be loved.

He finally said, "How is it possible to connect with women when I'm always abandoned by them? In my present life I was sent to a foster home. In the life we just saw I was abandoned, as I was when I was Sedeth. Life after life, abandonment is the theme.

"Why should I change my present existence, where I'm safe and secure, even though I'm holding onto my wife as if she were my mother? What's wrong with having one life of security?"

"Nothing," said Nur quietly. "If you're happy and satisfied, there's no reason to move on. Are you happy, Ronald? Is your soul satisfied? Is your soul feeling like a victorious warrior—or a warrior in terror?"

"That's a good question, Nur," answered Ronald, more soberly than I had ever heard him. "I never knew there was another self, one without terror. I never understood that terror could be changed, that life could be designed by oneself. I've become aware that terror freezes the organism. I've been frozen stiff."

From the distance I listened to this more honest Ronald, who I felt could be redeemed if he persisted on pursuing rectification.

"I'm stiff all over, Kendra, and I don't let too much in. My life at home feels safe because my wife's always the same. We've become entombed with one another." He paused, then said fervently, "What luck that you and I met, Kendra. I would have remained in my entombment forever."

"Are you saying 'thanks,' Ronald?"

"I'm saying it for the moment, Kendra. I'm not saying more than that."

Ronald was quiet for a long time. He finally asked timidly if he could spend the night with me. I was astonished. "What happened to your six o'clock curfew?"

"I'm bypassing it," he answered. "I'd like to be close to you. No sex or attempt at it. I just want to be near you. Is that agreeable?"

"I don't know, Ronald," I demurred, consulting my male and female identities, who consented after a few moments. "It'll be okay with me as long as you let your wife know you're staying with me, so I'm not called during the night."

"I'll talk to her." He left the room to speak to her. When he returned, even though I was not physically present, I could tell by his weakened demeanor that she was extremely angered by his request.

"I can't do it now," he told me defeatedly. "I'll see you tomorrow."

"Good night, Ronald," I said calmly. "It will work out for the best."

He was grateful for my sensitivity. He said nothing more as we cut off our telepathic communication.

I stayed up late that night, banishing my own foppish male energy from myself by burning it out. I knew it was there, because Ronald's male energy was a part of my own male energy. I imagined a huge cauldron filled with an igniting substance which, when set on fire, was explosive. I put Ronald's unpalatable character, the one whose lifetime had unfolded before us today as an aspect of my male energy, into the fire until it disintegrated into ashes. The transmutation was fast; my unconscious had no resistance to destroying every part of it.

I then cleansed my entire body by imagining the four elements—fire, earth, air, and water—streaming through me, removing any debris left over from this character. I bathed, went to bed, and slept soundly.

In the morning I reorganized my male and female energies, observing them as I stood before a mirror. I energized both the male and female genders until I felt the male's power and the female's balanced state.

I did my daily exercise by walking on a dirt road in the form of my new male energy. Since he was more difficult to capture, I spent a good deal of time incorporating him, moving from and speaking from his power.

I did the same with the female energy, making certain she was in her own appropriate part of me and not taking over the male strength.

On my way home, I strove to experience the balance between the two energies. When I had mastered the physicality of their energies, I spoke as the female, then as the male. They then dialogued with one another.

By the time I arrived back at my house, I felt synchronized.

Oh, God, I thought—with thanksgiving for the clearer, balanced me who was emerging. Thou art bountiful. What other growth will be forthcoming today?

19

Will I Ever Get It Right?

I was at my computer, trying to finish the manuscript, which had a strict deadline. I heard the phone ring. It was Ronald.

"Do you still like me, Kendra?" he asked sheepishly.

"Yes," I told him. "What's happened since last night?"

"I'm in a war. A war with myself. It's about whether to move forward or to not move forward. Part of me wants to. Another part is terrified."

"I know that conflict," I said reassuringly. "I go through it all the time. Living means struggling—struggling to gain more consciousness. You're at the beginning of that struggle. I know it's not easy, particularly since your wife resists looking into herself. In addition, the two of you have been feeding off each other's unbalanced energies for years, creating a symbiotic dependency. I know you don't want to hurt her, but sometimes staying in something that's devoid of the sap of life is more deadly and frightening than moving forward. That's been my experience. But it doesn't necessarily have to be yours. However, you've been abandoned in two past lives so far. What do you think destiny is telling you?"

"Destiny is giving me hell—that's clear," he acknowledged.

"Have you ever wondered," I asked him, "why you repeat your theme of abandonment so often?"

After a long silence he admitted, "I suppose it's because I've never faced it. I've never been alone long enough to find out what being alone feels like. I've managed to hook onto another woman, one way or another."

"I agree with you, Ronald," I told him, happy he was this honest with himself. "I'm beginning to feel that if you decide to leave your wife, it might be a bad idea to rush immediately into another relationship. That includes ours, even though we care deeply for one another. Perhaps you've got to test the waters of living by staying by yourself for a while, experiencing your male in the world—how he'll behave, other than by serving a woman. Has that possibility ever occurred to you?"

"No, but it's a good idea," he responded. "Frankly, though, it terrifies me."

"There must be reasons from other lives why being alone terrifies you," I told him, like Sherlock Holmes intrigued by a mystery. "Call on Nur to guide you to find another life. Do it by yourself. I've got a deadline and can't be with you until it's been met."

"Okay, but I'll miss you. Keep one ear open in case I get stuck, won't you?" he asked earnestly.

I couldn't resist his request.

"One ear is what you're getting, my love. Now let me get going with my project while you do yours."

I hung up the phone, smiling at the potential purity of his nature and my love for him.

I returned to my computer and kept one ear alert for Ronald's voice.

"Nur, Nur, I need you. Please appear. I'm ready to find another life."

"I'm here, Ronald, ready for you."

"Please, can't we contact a male who's strong, with balls, one who has conviction about himself? How I need such an experience! I know you can't manufacture such a life. I know it wouldn't be valid unless it were true. But show me someone who's more of a man. I don't care what else he does, just let me find a male with balls."

"A man with balls? You mean a male energy that's strong, able to love a woman the way she should be loved? A confident male?" questioned Nur.

"Yes!" Ronald pleaded, waiting for the first image to appear in the waterfall and rainbow.

I smiled with pleasure as I heard him search for a stronger male. With only part of my attention focused on his story— the other part on my manuscript—I heard that Ronald's past-life encounter was with a strong, burly, handsome man, plotting his escape from an unjust imprisonment. His name was Peter. He was determined to return to his beautiful wife in a village that was three weeks' travel by foot from the prison.

One day Peter makes his escape from the fields where he and the other prisoners have been laboring. He's armed with a weapon he had secretly devised during his long confinement. He had hidden it in a spot where he could easily retrieve it at the time of his escape.

Weapon in hand, Peter runs from the prison until he finds a cave. He crawls into it and sleeps. He kills animals for food. He continues his homeward journey until he finds himself in his village. Peter rushes toward his house and peers at it from behind thick bushes. He sees his beautiful wife taking water in a large bucket from their well. He's filled with emotion and would have run recklessly to her, had he not remembered that the neighbors, who had unjustly accused him before, would return him to the authorities.

From his hiding place, Peter calls to her softly. "Marla, my love. Marla. Don't be startled. Don't look up. It's Peter, your husband. Go into the house. I'll meet you inside. Go quickly."

She does what he says. When they meet inside, he needs a long time to convince his wife that he's real and at home. Finally, when she stops crying and understands that he's not a mirage, they love each other passionately.

"That's more like it!" said Ronald, chuckling with delight. "I'm so hungry to see some kind of courage shown by my male nature." He breathed like a man reborn.

Good! I thought. I'll let him go through his life by himself. If I don't do my work now, I'll be in trouble. "Ronald, you're on your own," I told him.

"Okay, but don't abandon me altogether."

"Abandon you?" I chuckled.

I returned to my manuscript, trying to shut Ronald out, but that was difficult. I must admit I was curious about the stronger male in him. I listened to bits and pieces of this particular past life, while at the same time I tried to stay focused on my work. I heard that they left the village before he was detected.

Marla and Peter settle in the middle of a thick forest, a long distance from their former home. In the forest he builds a cabin and Marla cultivates a garden. They're blissful for a while. When the crops fail, however, she becomes angry and blames her husband for her uncomfortable life. She turns into a shrew, whose nature he's never seen before.

One day she leaves on horseback, never looking back. Peter is bewildered. He talks to himself, trying to make sense of her departure and his life:

> *I was loving, caring, devoted.*
> *I found an ingenious way to*
> *escape from prison. I'm a good*
> *carpenter. I took care of your*
> *needs. I made love to you until*
> *you were satisfied.*
> *What's wrong?*
>
> *My mother left my home in the*
> *same way,*
> *never looking back.*
> *My drunken father didn't stop*
> *her.*
> *I couldn't stop her.*
> *I was too little.*
>
> *My father then drank himself*
> *to death.*
> *I'm alone.*
> *I fend for myself.*
> *I'm lonely—*
> *so despairing.*
>
> *I meet Marla.*
> *She's the redress for all*
> *my losses.*
>
> *But then she leaves,*
> *and my loneliness*
> *overwhelms me.*
>
> *Many weeks have passed*
> *since Marla's departure.*
> *I'm still in a daze.*
> *I go to the village inn*
> *and drink until I feel*
> *no pain.*

A young, beautiful woman
approaches me.
I look at her longingly.
She flirts and teases
until I become crazed
with passion.

She comes to my cabin.
I want her!
Oh, how I want her!

She plays recklessly with
my longing and my need to
be loved.
She scorns me and walks out
of the cabin—

like my mother did,
like Marla.

I left the computer, screaming to Ronald, "Bring her back! Go after her! Don't let her do this to you! Don't let yourself fall into despair. Fight for what you want. Don't let the woman make a little boy out of you. Fight!"

I was nearly crazed by Peter's passivity. It was my male's passivity, my father's, Ronald's, other men's as well.

Ronald yelled at me, "Don't you see how much stronger he is, Kendra? What do you want from him?"

"He's stronger," I shouted back at him, "but he's so filled with despair because he doesn't have the woman's love, he's willing to die."

"How do you know that?" asked Ronald. "He's such a better specimen of a man than the last past-life character. Why can't you be satisfied with Peter the way he is?"

"Because he's so dependent on a woman and still caught in that trap. I'll bet he kills himself!"

"I'll bet he doesn't!" said Ronald, satisfied by the image of a male not overcome by terror.

When Nur asked us if we wished to continue, Ronald told her yes—emphatically—feeling certain he would be proved right. He was still irate when he told me, "Nothing is ever enough for you. You want everything all the time. You have no tolerance, no compassion. None."

"What's wrong with wanting everything? What's wrong with wanting a full self? What's wrong with wanting the perfection of God? You've accepted a crumb here and a crumb there. You're worth more. I want more for you, more from you, more, more, more, so we can join and be balanced. Oh, God! I feel like an obsessive-compulsive!"

We were quiet for a long time. I returned to my computer, steaming. From our telepathic distance I heard:

I lie in my bed
for days, looking
at the ceiling.

I don't eat.
I don't drink.
Sleep is unnecessary.

My mind ruminates:
I'm not wanted.
I'm alone.
I feel worthless.

These thoughts become
a mindless recitation.
I lie on my back
week after week
until one day
I rise and
go to my weapon.
I look at it,
my eyes tearing.

"You're my steadfast
friend. You've seen me through
many crises.
You're going to do one
last service for me."

I point the blade in the
direction of
my heart.

A howl of despair comes
from my throat.

"Marla,
you left me.
Why?"

There was a profound silence. Ronald wept. "Will I ever get it right, Kendra?"

"You will, my darling, you will," I answered, totally consumed by his pain.

20
Individuation

I was deeply affected by the tragedy of Ronald's latest male life. It brought back memories of the despairing moments on my own journey toward wholeness. I recalled those intense moments, which had totally depleted me of energy. I recalled my feelings of hopelessness about life, which made the thought of death welcome. I remembered that until another, more positive connection is made, the pull to stay in despair is monumental.

Back then, in a flash, I'd forgotten my angelic origin. In a flash, I'd become overwhelmed by others' cruelties. In a flash, others' rejections had returned me to a state of not being wanted—of wishing I were dead. In a flash, I became a zero—nonexistent, a being without meaning.

I remembered remaining in such a state until a therapist pulled me out of it. The therapist's understanding nature gave me the feeling that someone cared. He said, "Hi, I like you. You're not all the horrible things you're thinking about yourself. You're a striking, interesting human being."

I remembered falling into those pits of loneliness and despair on my journey, until still another voice emerged. It was not a friend's, nor a therapist's. It was an inner voice, speaking more clearly than any human voice. I realized then that perhaps destiny's plan was to deny me human contact so I would strive more arduously for contact with the celestial beings. Why else would my life be so devoid of closeness with other people? The universe is benign, not punitive. Was this happening by design?

I struggled to reach their level. I struggled to believe what they told me. I'm still struggling to trust their voices rather than human voices. I'm struggling to live in their world, with my feet on the earth; to be rectifying, always seeking balance. I'm struggling to create a balance between my female and male energies, because that balance will bring me closer to my Godself.

I'm grateful to Ronald for his "visitation" with Nur. I receive it as a gift of the soul. Ronald is my male self. He's in the process of changing. He will have to fight to rise to a higher self. Until he does, we remain unbalanced. I must therefore develop my own male and leave his male energy behind.

Like Ronald, I was deprived of nurturance from my parents. Other human beings became substitute parents. I expected them to give to me unconditionally. No efforts can satisfy such deprivation. At present, Ronald still looks to his wife to fill the void. But no human being can fill that void. Only when this truth is recognized will the needy person be forced to look within for answers and satisfaction. It is a time of *individuation*, the process described by that remarkable word coined by Carl Jung. Individuation: separation from the parents to find one's intrinsic self.

I thought of Jesus' individuation process, as told in the Bible:

> His parents, Mary and Joseph,
> could not find Him for three
> days, while in the city of
> Jerusalem.

> Jesus had found His divine voice
> at the age of thirteen and begun
> teaching in the temple.

> When Mary and Joseph finally
> located their son, they rebuked Him
> for giving them anxiety and sorrow.

> His response:

> "You are not my real father and
> mother.
> My real father is in heaven."

> He had found His individuated
> Self,
> His divinity.

This was His true Self,
a Self whose voice became His
primary voice.

I knew that Ronald and I were on different rungs of the ladder. I also knew I would not allow myself to be held back by waiting for him to catch up.

21
The Rungs of the Ladder

We met again two weeks later. I had processed Ronald's last life, transmuting my own dependent male energy into good energy, which I then balanced with my female energy.

I was in the basement of my home when Ronald breezed past me through the magic door and asked me how I was. In his next breath he made sure to let me know that he had extricated himself from his dependency on women.

I mumbled, "Good, Ronald. I'm glad to hear it."

"That last life as Peter was helpful because I now see I can be sexual, burly, and courageous," he told me, strutting around the room much like a matador would before he assailed the bull with his deadly sword.

I noticed he had incorporated Peter's physicality. Apparently I was the charging bull he had to subdue, and he was intensely focused on this mission.

I was amused but said nothing as I submitted to his imagery. I watched him indulge in his newfound power, realizing that trying on all energies is a way of discovering oneself.

"How do you like me? I'm pretty strong, am I not?"

"A real macho man!" I replied. "You're sensational!"

"That I am," he said with confidence, taking me in his arms. "I missed you, my love," he whispered as he nibbled on my earlobe. It was difficult for me to restrain hysterical laughter.

"Have you been watching movies from the fifties?" I blurted out. I mimicked him—"My love, my love"—and swooned in his arms.

We did a tango.

"My love," I howled with laughter. "Oh, Ronald, you're priceless. What a bull! Let me feel your biceps." He lifted his right arm, flexing that mountainous muscle.

"Ouch!" he cried, "you're pressing too hard. Press gently." He showed me how, by kissing my own biceps, planting delicate kisses. He continued kissing my arm until he arrived at my neck, which he bit hard enough to make me scream.

"Ronald!" I yelled.

He kissed me, suctioning my lips until there was no breath left in my body. I begged for mercy.

"I'm pretty strong and dangerous, *n'est-ce pas?*"

"*Bien sûr!*"

We rolled on the floor, laughing until we cried.

"Oh, Ronald, it's good to see you. I missed you, too. We play so well together."

We stayed on the floor, embracing and feeling close. I told him I would be going on vacation the following day.

He immediately became despondent. "You're going away without me?" His voice was petulant.

"Ronald, stop leading me on. You couldn't and wouldn't leave your wife to go on vacation with me, would you? So I'm taking a trip to the West Coast alone. I can combine business with pleasure. It'll just be for a week."

"I miss you already," he moaned. "Promise to call me every day!"

"Yes, baby," I answered sardonically. "Not once a day, but three times a day. Will that please you? I'm sure it will please your wife."

"Sorry, Kendra. I'm just telling you how your leaving affects me."

"Okay," I said, feeling irritated that I was once again in the position of stopping my feelings because the man was proclaiming irresponsibly. Do I always have to be grounded for the other person as well as for myself?

I continued with my silent, despondent thoughts. Isn't there a male in this universe who knows he wants me and pursues me with desire? These thoughts flashed in and out of my mind, making me more aware than ever how much I needed contact with a stronger male.

"Let's call on Nur to hear what she has to say about your last life and where you are in general," I suggested diplomatically.

"Nur, where are you?" we asked.

"I'm here," she announced quietly. "How did you process your last character, Ronald?"

"I'm something else," said Ronald. "I didn't realize how important it is to find all those pieces of the puzzle that are called 'you.' I've heard Kendra say this many times, but until I experienced it for myself, I didn't get it."

The last life gave you an awareness of your physical and sexual strength—of yourself when you lack terror. You've been wishing to conquer that terror in this life. Recognize that you have the capacity to do so. In the life as Peter, you were resourceful, loving, and devoted, but too dependent on the woman. You're still in that state today."

"I know," said Ronald, "but I can master that, knowing about the Peter character in me."

"Remember," Nur continued, *"that as you gain more information about your selves, you can slowly process what you have learned and reorganize your female and male energies. In doing so, you prepare yourself for ascension to the highest places. Has this not been your experience, Kendra?"* Nur asked, turning to me.

"Yes, climbing up a steep ladder is hard. In climbing to the next rung, I've often lost my footing and fallen several rungs below. When that happened I became immersed in life's meaningless pursuits, lost to my true self. I would remain in such a state until a dawning light in my consciousness reminded me that I could take the next step. When I did move forward, I regretted the inertia I had succumbed to, which had kept me in a static place. But I understood intuitively, as I experienced each ascension and falling back, that sooner or later I would find the right consciousness to propel me upward."

"Are you telling me that I might get stuck in this Peter character?" asked Ronald, annoyed.

"No, Ronald. I'm saying that growth requires a conscious effort. It's an arduous journey, needing courage, fortitude, and relentless desire to pursue the self. Such has been my experience. Yours will be yours—different from mine."

"You bet it'll be mine," said Ronald, peeved that Nur had taken the spotlight away from him and given it to me; peeved that his Peter character was not male enough for both women; and peeved that they both advised him to keep moving forward.

From that moment, we spoke little. The atmosphere became tense. I couldn't and didn't wish to placate him. I was tired.

When it was clear neither of us would budge from our emotional positions, he came to me, kissed me lightly on both sides of my mouth, pressed me to him, and told me to have a good trip.

"I will," I replied, hurt and angered, disappointed that once again I was not being fully met. He opened our magic door, and slipped out into the night, like a little boy who had come to someone's home, gotten into the cookie jar, and eaten his fill.

I locked the door and listened to his car roar away. At the same time I heard the grandfather clock strike its emphatic six chimes.

"Ahuuh," I thought. "Ahuuh!"

That night I dreamed a significant dream—a dream of a vital, strong, massive female. An Amazon. She was of gargantuan proportions, with numerous teats on her chest. Behind her stood a Herculean male. He picked her up and set her on his lap. She placed her hands around his head, helping him suck from her breasts. As they fused, wisdom and consciousness enfolded the two beings, bringing them into oneness.

When I awakened the next morning and stood before my bathroom sink, I felt as though the top of the sink, which ordinarily touched my lower abdomen, had sunk to my knees. I felt enormous.

I am enormous, I thought,
proudly accepting it as a
fact I no longer wanted to
deny.

I am at last a true Amazon,
Nur!
One for the coming age.
An Aquarian Amazon!

22

We Reap
What We Sow

I arrived on the West Coast the following day. It was beautiful: palm trees and blue skies, warm weather, and red-tiled roofs. When I entered the office of my literary agent, I was greeted with flattering warmth and interest. The agent had submitted my manuscript to a publisher who had been interested in it for the past year. Negotiations, with my approval, had been concluded. I was told the contract would be ready to sign in a few hours. The agent wondered if I would mind waiting. Would I mind waiting? I repeated to myself. I've been waiting a lifetime to be published. I'll wait for the rest of my life if need be!

After receiving many congratulations and settling plans for editing my work, I sat in a restaurant eating lunch, pinching myself over and over. Is this happening to me? Is this real? Why did it take so long to happen? What do they see now that they didn't see six months ago? Then they had procrastinated. Now, they have a contract ready to be signed. I wondered if my wholeness—my strong male and my fruitful female—resonated so powerfully that it had become an irresistible force?

Someone tapped me on the shoulder as I was finishing dessert. I turned around to see, towering above me, a male as beautifully fascinating as a sculpture of a Greek god. He smiled, his dark, handsome face lit from within by a warm glow. He introduced himself as Jeremy Braun, saying that my agent had told him where he could find me. He asked if he could join me. I consented.

Jeremy was a film producer. He told me he read my manuscript a year ago, had never forgotten it, and was considering making a film based on it. "Are you interested?" he asked.

I gulped. "Am I interested?" I repeated, my face beaming with excitement. "I'd be in heaven if you did."

"In heaven?" he asked. "Is that where you live most of the time?"

I was taken aback by his question. After a moment's thought, I answered, "I long to have that connection most of the time, but I can't always get there. What about you?"

"It's the same for me," Jeremy answered with a note of sadness. "I often get lost in Earth's reality and forget the other exists. I've been struggling to stay in both worlds, but it's not so easy."

We looked into one another's eyes and beyond them.

"I'm divorced, looking for the right partner," he told me hesitantly, clearly wondering if he was being too presumptuous.

"I'm looking for the right partner, too," I responded quietly. "I've been divorced a long time."

"How long are you staying in town?"

"I leave tonight," I told him, as if in the flow of a stream named destiny.

"But you'll have to return soon. And you'll have to stay a long time, because you'll be participating in the entire procedure—the scriptwriting, casting, shooting."

"I guess you're right. I have to return and stay a long time," I answered, in a whirl of confusion and jubilation.

"I feel as though I know you. My heart tells me I want you," he said cautiously.

"You do?" I asked, struggling to keep my male and female balanced. "I want to be wanted more than anything in this world. I want it as much as I want to be published and to have my manuscript turned into a film."

"I can give it all to you," he smiled. "How about a date in two weeks when you come back? We can coordinate work with getting to know one another."

"I'll be here." I looked into Jeremy's dark eyes. As I gazed, in my mind I saw the titanic male and female figures of my dream.

They were moving around one another, silently—breathing, sensing, feeling, knowing.

An Aquarian-age Amazon. A fulfilled warrioress, united with her warrior.

He took me to a taxi, pressed my hand strongly, and said, "It's a deal."

When I returned home, I answered the many messages left on my machine. None had come from Ronald.

You missed the boat, Ronald, I thought with bittersweet regret and goodwill. I want to be wanted—as God wants me, as I want me. It's possible now, because I have my female and male energies. Then I said aloud, "Thanks for your part in helping me to wholeness."

Kendra's Prayer

I have spoken to You, God.

Thou art bountiful.

Thou workest in mysterious ways.

Thy Will be done.

Thank You.

Amen.

Guide to Terms Used in This Book

Bioenergetics: "A therapeutic technique to help a person get back together with his body and to help him enjoy to the fullest degree possible the life of the body. This emphasis on the body includes sexuality. . . as well as breathing, moving, feeling and self-expression." (*Bioenergetics*, Alexander Lowen, M.D., p.43. Coward, McCann & Geoghegan, Inc., NY, 1975.) This therapeutic modality was founded by Alexander Lowen, M.D., and John Pierrakos, M.D.

Armoring: A term coined by Wilhelm Reich, founder of Vegetotherapy, the root of Bioenergetics. Armoring refers to the muscular tension in the body that provides a shield against painful and threatening emotional experiences. The organism can begin its armoring from the time of birth, if not before.

Symbiosis: The paralyzed emotional state of two people who cannot separate themselves from each other because they have each pasted images of their parents onto the other. In such a state neither person lives from himself/herself. This superimposed state serves to keep the psyche alive, since living through another gives the person an identity.

Reflectivism: A term coined by the author. I believe we choose our parents prenatally in order to learn whatever lessons we need for growth. It is important for us to accept that we are a reflection of them, for then we can face, accept, and surmount our own limitations. Reflectivism is a concept of self-responsibility and self-absolution.

Imaging: A process by which we palpate certain areas of the body. When the physical part in question is sufficiently alive, the seeker meditates on the area to elicit information. In this book, both Kendra and Ronald palpate the upper energy centers, which enables them to contact Nur, their higher self.

The process can become clairvoyant, clairsentient, and clairaudient.

Past Lives: Much has been written about the fact or fiction of other lives. I will not enter into that debate here, for I am convinced that other lives, whether metaphorical or real, are facts of existence and give a person a larger vision of himself/herself. This is so for both Ronald and Kendra, who learn about aspects of themselves they might never have encountered without such probing. When experienced deeply and in connection with one's present life, such insights into a deeper nature will open doors to a self that might otherwise remain clogged and buried.

Female/Male Energies: In the nature of all of us reside the female and male energies. When the consciousness embraces this concept, a person can extricate himself/herself from parental influences, either wanted or unwanted. When purified, these energies can join the Godself, creating a wholeness that is everyone's quest. (In the classical sense, and in my own perception as well, the female energy is housed on the left side of the body, the male on the right side of the body.)

Godself: A state that can be achieved when the female/male energies are balanced. Then the person is able to connect to the wholeness of God, separated from parental influences and totally involved in her/his own essence.

Anneliese Widman, Ph.D., author of *Aquarian Amazon,* has also written two other books—***Rage at God:*** *Ascending to Reunion* and ***My Female, My Male, My Self, and God:*** *A Modern Woman in Search of Her Soul.* Contact Dr. Widman by e-mail at **info@shortcuttogodself.com** and, for complete information, see her Web site at **www.shortcuttogodself.com**. She can also be reached in care of:

Pentland Press, Inc.
5122 Bur Oak Circle
Raleigh, NC 27612 USA
(800) 948-2786
FAX (919) 781-9042
e-mail: **info@pentlandpressusa.com**